SHROUD

From
Shroud Publishing LLC

You are holding a limited edition small press publication in your hands. This book is a result of hard work and creative effort. Enjoy it and celebrate the possibility of all things.

Designed and Printed in the USA

SP
Shroud Publishing

www.shroudmagazine.com

First Edition
First Printing April 30, 2008
Copyright 2008 Shroud Publishing
All Rights Reserved

The individual copyrights of the respective authors herein reverted back to the original copyright holder upon publication.

Cover Art by Thomas Straub
http://www.myspace.com/hauntedart

ISBN: 978-0-9801870-2-1

Shroud Publishing LLC
#59295
P.O. Box 7775
San Francsico, CA 94120-7775

or

121 Mason Rd.
Milton, NH 03851

Shroud #2 March/April

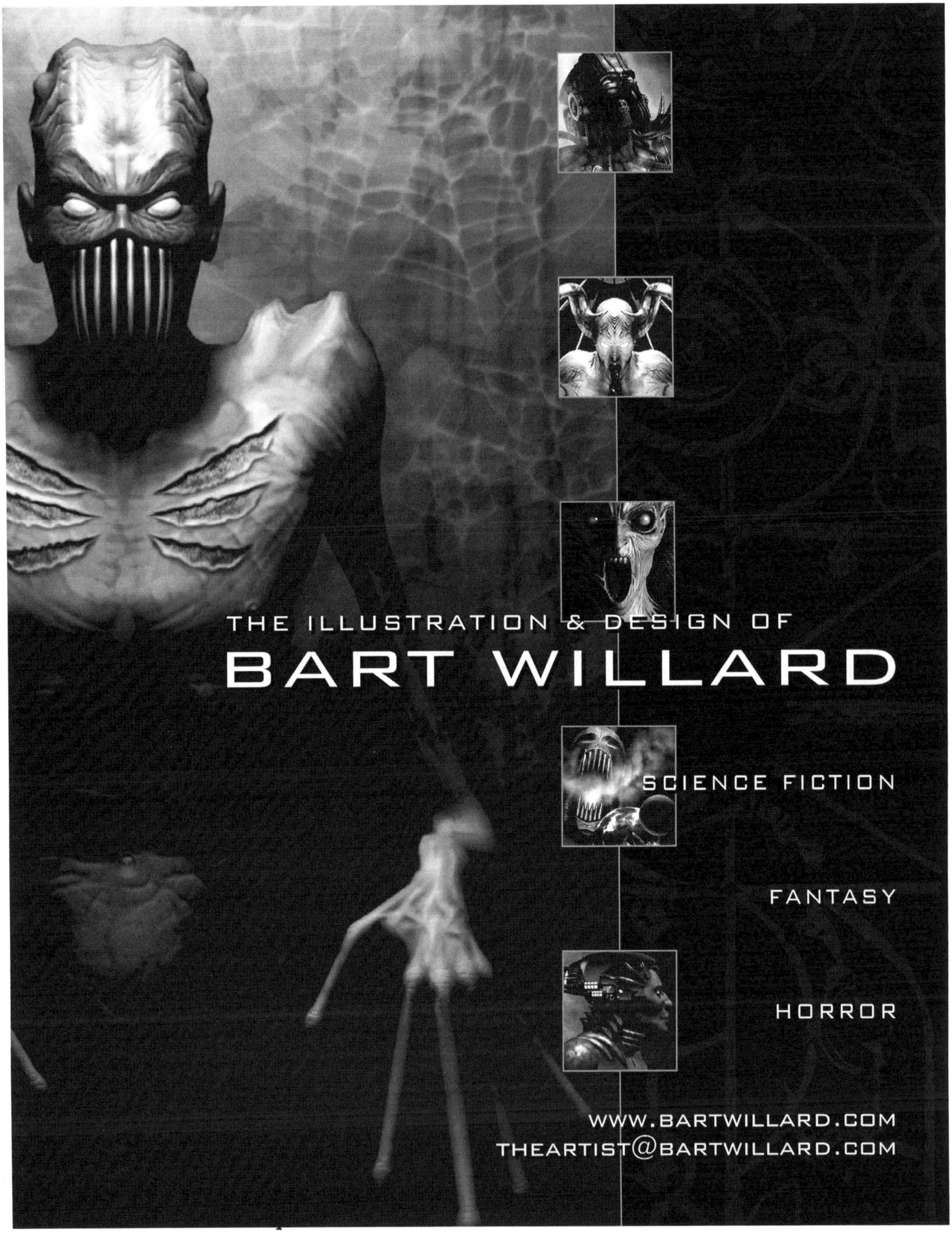

THE ILLUSTRATION & DESIGN OF
BART WILLARD

SCIENCE FICTION

FANTASY

HORROR

WWW.BARTWILLARD.COM
THEARTIST@BARTWILLARD.COM

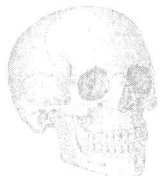
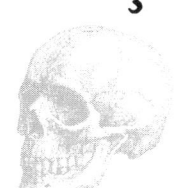

Issue# 2, March/April 2008
SHROUD
The Journal of Dark Fiction and Art

Shroud Magazine
Issue 2, March/April 2008

Publisher
Shroud Publishing LLC

Editor
Timothy P. Deal

Assistant Editor
Christa Miller

Marketing
Jennifer N. Deal

Layout and Design
Dale Mythito

Contributing Editors
I.E. Lester
Shawn Oetzel

Contributing Artists
Thomas Straub
Emily Tolson
Dean Spencer
Malcolm McClinton

Cover Art
Thomas Straub

ISSN
1940-7025

Copyright (c) 2007 by Shroud Publishing LLC. Individual works are copyright (c) 2007 by their respective creators. All rights reserved.

Fiction

AMUSE-BOUCHE, Colleen Anderson	6
HARD SOUP, Steve Vernon	8
BEGGAR'S BLESSING, Marie Brennan	11
HAVEN, Kealan Patrick Burke	25
PINK ELEPHANT, Nathaniel Lambert	33
HOME, Maura McHugh	37
THE THING IN THE WOODS, Nate Kenyon	43
BE THE DARKNESS, Tom Piccirilli and Ken Bruen	52
ANKLE BITERS, Christa M. Miller	71
MYSPACE FLASH FICTION CONTEST #1	75

Nonfiction

1968: THE YEAR THAT CHANGED HORROR, Peter Guitierrez	16
TIM LEBBON, an interview, Paul Kane	21
THE BLOODLUST OF ELIZABETH BATHORY, by I.E. Lester	66
THE HAUNTED ART OF THOMAS STRAUB, Tim Deal	87

Books

DUMA KEY, by Stephen King	60
FIRES RISING, by Michael Laimo	61
GOING BACK, by Tony Richards	61
DALTON QUAYLE RIDES OUT, by Paul Kane	62
HORRORS BEYOND 2, edited by William Jones	63

Film

THE GREAT BEAST, by Marie O'Regan	81
THE EYE, Shawn Oetzel	83
JOSHUA, Shawn Oetzel	84
GAMERS, Tim Deal	85

Extras

PUZZLED: Horror Author Word Search, I.E. Lester	91

Whispers, AND OTHER UTTERANCES
Letters From Our Readers

Shroud was happy to receive these reactions to the availability of our premiere issue. We'd really appreciate hearing from you as well. Please email us at editor@shroudmagazine.com. We would sincerely love to hear your ideas for making Shroud better. You can also join our forum at www.shroudmagazine.com. Thank you!

Tim,

I just wanted to let you know, I finished issue one of SHROUD about three minutes ago, and you have a hell of a magazine on your hands! Of course, I'd say that about any magazine with Tom Piccirilli in it (to say nothing of the interview with Brian Keene), but as fantastic as "Circling" was, I liked Michael Laimo's "Layover" better. I also enjoyed the article about Burke and Hare (a favorite subject of mine) and Indio's "Lobotomy Screen" is a ghastly work of art.

So, uh . . . [scratch my arm and jitter] when's issue two coming out?

-John Bruni

***

Dear Tim & Jenn,

Sorry for not writing earlier. I really enjoyed reading Issue #1 of Shroud Magazine and I am looking forward to reading the next one.

I knew I would like the stories when I read your editorial and you mention your preference for "fantasy stories set in real, identifiable locations." That's also why I was never satisfied with other short stories magazines I am reading, until I read yours.

Please let me know when issue #2 is ready!

I loved the stories of Tom Piccirilli, Catherine Knutsson and Michael Laimo.

I.E. Lester's article was very interesting and I hope we will see more pieces of the kind in future issues.

Indio's drawing was beautifully disturbing.

I also wanted to recommend a new author (you may already know him). His name is Charlie Huston and he writes fast-paced, violent novels you will probably enjoy as much as I do.

He gave an interesting twist to the vampire story (I don't usually like vampire stories, but this is good shit). It's set in present day NYC. Here are the titles in order: *Already Dead; No Dominion; Half the Blood of Brooklyn.*

He also did a great noir trilogy equally as good: *Caught Stealing; Six Bad Things; A Dangerous Man.*

The guy is great and I invite you to visit his website: www.pulpnoir.com.

English is not my first language (me French) and I hope this email makes sense.

I am looking forward to reading Issue #2 of Shroud!

All best,
-Yann

We'd love to hear from you! Send your ideas, suggestions, criticism and praise to editor@shroudmagazine.com

From The Editor: The Joy of Fear And the Gnashing of Teeth
Tim Deal

In the short few months that Shroud has existed, a number of similar publications have closed their doors or otherwise ceased operations. Of these, many were Web-based publications available only in HTML or .PDF. The rapid demise of these publications—especially those that did not carry the weighty costs of a print entity—underscores the transient nature of the speculative fiction market. This fact is made particularly thought-provoking when one considers the number of writers that depend upon the continued existence of reliable periodical markets in order to pay their power bills, fuel their cars, or to put food on their tables.

Many have argued that that widespread proliferation of Web 2.0 tools has significantly lowered the barriers to entry in publishing endeavors. As a result, a glut of publishing entities have quickly sprouted up only to ultimately fail as they ran out of money, collapsed beneath the effort, or fell at the hands of their founders who eventually loss interest. Any casual observer of horror periodical markets would not flinch at the diminutive life cycle of new publications. It is a well-accepted but sad fact that magazines fail, and when magazines fail, writers do not get paid.

I mention these things because they represent some of the lessons I have learned in my short career as a publisher. The first thing I realized upon embarking on this wonderful journey was that many, many others came before me, and that most of them ultimately crashed and burned along with their dreams of a massive subscriber base, a shelf full of Bram Stoker Awards, and a fat bank account heavily laden with advertiser dollars. So it goes, again and again.

As I monitored writers' discussions at the HWA's member message boards, I quickly learned that the rapid spawn and demise of these magazines is a significant source of disruption that creates untold frustration to professional horror writers, not to mention the scores of subscribers left in the lurch. The bottom line of these observations is that the creation of any publishing projects, by its very nature, creates an eco system of writers, editors, artists, advertiser and readers around it. As a result, such an undertaking should never be taken lightly.

I write this during a period of economic hardship for all of us. Despite assurances to the contrary from the current lame duck administration, we are experiencing a period of economic recession that has vastly tightened discretionary spending. Shelling out five or six bucks for a magazine is a luxury that many cannot readily afford.

I think it absolutely critical to soldier on and get these fantastic stories in front of an audience who appreciates them. I did not launch Shroud as a whim or a hobby, but as something that I dearly and truly hope will become a legacy. I purposefully placed myself in a position where I would be exposed to and surrounded by like-minded creative souls, and I did so because anything less could not make me as fulfilled.

On a lighter note, you will notice that this issue is in a new trim size. Please let me know what you think. Although we are only two issues in, I think you would all agree with me—this is our best issue yet. ;)

Shroud Flash Fiction

AMUSE-BOUCHE
n. Fr. (it) entertains (the) mouth

By Colleen Anderson

Elena leaned forward, on the edge of her seat, smiling at me. "I've waited a long time, my petite chou." I said nothing, no longer interested in that flash of laughter in her eyes or those deceiving dimples on her cheeks. I closed my eyes for a moment's rest.

"Uh uh." She smacked the whip in her hand. "I want you to be part of this. No wandering off." We both knew it a hollow threat. It wasn't the whip she would use.

Elena leaned close, staring into my eyes. "I hope you don't mind if I savor our time." She licked my ear, her tongue pointedly exploring each groove and whorl.

All I could do was moan as my mind slid to that moment I'd met her at the house party. She had impishly raised her eyebrow after Ben introduced us and said, "Ooh, I'd just love to eat you up. You're so cute." I'd laughed, embarrassed and intrigued. A flush crept up her cheeks. "I hope this isn't too much for you." She kissed my lips, nibbling the edge and closing her eyes for a moment.

I swallowed, taking deep breaths through my nose. My thoughts traveled back to our day in the park. Elena had woven her way through the stark branches that clawed at the stormy sky as if tearing it with skeletal fingers. Then she'd disappeared when I had looked away. I called, looking through arm-thick trees, then scurrying, calling again, confused. "Elena!" I shook my head and walked toward the darker copse of trees and brush. At the edge I peered in, shivering at the darkness. I looked behind once more, and there she was, petite, muffled in scarf and hat, staring at me. "Where'd you go?"

She had continued staring at me for a few minutes until I had finally penetrated her private world. Now I tried to find mine as I returned to the present. Elena ran her tongue between my fingers, sucking on the ends. I hadn't noticed. She smiled softly.

> *Elena leaned close, staring into my eyes. "I hope you don't mind if I savor our time."*

"I really do appreciate you." I shivered and groaned, pulling at the ropes, but she had tied me well. "Sweety, play fair. You men always come first. Now it's my turn." Her damned sparkling eyes on me, she licked her way up my cock. I felt nothing but the gorge rise and I swallowed several times. Her full, burgundy lips kissed its length, then closed around the tip as it slid into her mouth. She bit, grinding her perfect teeth together as she severed the head. Chewing it down, she wriggled side to side, her other hand between her legs.

I glared hate. She reached toward the bowl. Instead, she stood and sauntered up to me. "Don't worry, babe. I save the best till last." She tapped my head. Then she went back to the bowl and picked up my lips. She gave me that look again, as she had in the woods, no longer smiling.

◇◇◇◇◇

Colleen Anderson's fiction and poetry has appeared in over 100 publications such as Chizine, Talebones, Amazing, Dreams of Decadence and the Open Space anthology in which "Hold Back the Night" received several nominations and two honorable mentions in the Year's Best anthologies.

Indulge Your Dark Appetites...

Grab Your Favorite Blanky and Light a Fire.
Get Lost in a World of
MYSTERY, SUSPENSE, AND HORROR

Order today
at
WWW.SHROUDMAGAZINE.COM

Shroud Flash Fiction

Hard Soup

By Steve Vernon

I marinated the meat in the best red wine I could afford, for five days, with garlic and onion and bay leaf and a little stick of cinnamon, lots of cracked black pepper, and lots of tears.

On the fifth day I rubbed it with olive oil and browned it well in a hot pan. I kissed it for luck. Crane was right, it tasted bitter.

I carried the meat ceremoniously to a black metal roasting pan, which I'd beaten with a hammer into the rough shape of a coffin. I browned a sliced onion in the pan, added more tears, and a little butter for flavor.

Then I deglazed the fry pan with a bit of the marinade, stirring and scraping the caked-on bits from the pan, sluicing it with the juice for more flavor.

I poured the contents into the coffin-roaster, covering the meat just a little over half way. I stuck the coffin-roaster into a slow oven, set to 300. Nice and slow, everything took time, let the hurting leak on out.

I added the insecticide last.

I served it in a valentine shaped bowl, bought especially for the occasion. I set her body in her chair across the table from me. The freezer kept her when I could not. Her chest hung open like a secret treasure box. She had a smile on her face. I'd placed it there, a finishing touch before placing her in the freezer.

Finishing nails.

> *I carried the meat ceremoniously to a black metal roasting pan, which I'd beaten with a hammer into the rough shape of a coffin.*

Then I spooned it up. Bitter, it tasted bitter, but no worse than finding your wife in bed with your best friend.

Heart meat is hard, unless you cook it properly. I ate it up, every last drop.

I bit my lip until the gag reflex stopped working, and waited to die.

If I'd timed it right, they'd find us together before she thawed. A frozen tableau, two hearts, one broken in my chest and one well braised in my belly.

Well done. Well done.

◇◇◇◇◇

Steve has written for The Horror Show, Cemetery Dance, Flesh & Blood, Dark Wisdom, Karl Edward Wagner's Year's Best Horror, Chthulhu Sex, Horror Garage, Hot Blood anthology and many other markets and magazines. He has a four author - four novella collection of weird western novellas featuring his writing along side of Brian Keene, Tim Lebbon and Tim Curran - due out from Cemetery Dance in late 2008 or early 2009

Malcolm McClinton

http://hangedmanstudio.blogspot.com/

"Beggar's Blessing" by Dean Spencer

Beggar's Blessing

by Marie Brennan

[Illustrated by Dean Spencer]

"We beggars come now to your door
Please help us, sir, the humble poor
Charity will fill your halls
Misers have nothing at all."

Snow had fallen the previous day and already turned to grey slush, but the flakes that now drifted from the sky promised to gild the dreariness with a new layer of white. To Enhardt, it was an unwelcome sight. The first snow of the year was a sign of winter's beginning, and every subsequent one reaffirmed that spring had not yet come.

He hated winter, and spent as much of the season as he could indoors, huddled by the fire, counting the days until warmth returned. His scarecrow body felt the cold in its joints, and all winter long he creaked around the house, muttering querulous complaints under his breath. Had he possessed servants, his behavior would have driven them to distraction, but Enhardt had neither maid nor manservant, and so he walked through his cold house alone.

This suited him. He disliked company, especially when he was in a sour mood, and his sour moods lasted all winter.

"Some wine can warm our frozen hands
Guarding them from winter winds
May you have ten times more next year
So we'll get wine again from here."

"Bright the night to you, sir, and may Naus Mannein bring you joy," she said, bobbing an awkward curtsy. "Might you have a bit of wine you could spare?"

When the knock came on his door, he scowled. Both the milk and the meat had been delivered already, and he expected no one else save Rinolf Tschauber, who managed his accounts. But Tschauber was not due to come for some time yet, and would never come early. He knew how Enhardt hated unexpected visitors.

For a moment Enhardt considered not answering. But it might be Tschauber, or it might be an important visitor. He rose from his chair, knees cracking, and went into the front hall.

The caller was not Tschauber, nor anyone else important. It was a young woman, her cheeks bright red from the cold, her hazel eyes peering out from under a fringe of untrimmed hair that had escaped her tattered bonnet. The rest of her clothing was in equally poor shape, being little more than layers of patched fabric.

"Bright the night to you, sir, and may Naus Mannein bring you joy," she said, bobbing an awkward curtsy. "Might you have a bit of wine you could spare?"

"Wine?" Enhardt stared at her. Then the rest of her words sank in. Naus Mannein—that damnable evening had come around again. A holiday, they called it. He considered it a bloody nuisance. "No. You can't have any wine."

"Please—haven't you got even a drop to spare?"

"Not for the likes of you." The freezing air was wrapping itself around Enhardt's ankles. He wanted her off his doorstep and gone. Usually they knew better than to come to his house. "I don't give food and drink to worthless layabouts."

She blanched, but kept trying. "I'd sing the Beggar's Blessing for you, sir."

"A bit of annoying song is no kind of payment for valuable stores," Enhardt snapped. "I don't want your blessing."

But—She looked confused. Had she never been refused charity before?

"It'll bring you good luck in the coming year."

"I've done quite well without it."

Her wide hazel eyes gazed at him with unexpected seriousness. "Fortunes change. Why take the chance? Do a small kindness, and maybe you'll reap a reward."

"Perhaps your fortunes have fallen, but I'm not so careless as to go the same way." Enhardt had plenty of money set by, plenty to spare. "I'll go on as I have, thank you. Good evening."

He started to shut the door, but she blocked it with one rag-wrapped foot. "There's a storm coming," she said, her eyes huge and fearful. "More snows, and bitter cold. The storm will come tonight. It will be a hard night, sir."

"Find work, and earn money for shelter," Enhardt suggested. "I understand that most of the prostitutes gather on Tumble Street. I wish you luck in your search for employment." A quick shove on the door made her stagger back, and Enhardt closed it in her face.

Naus Mannein. Enhardt's least favorite time of year. In the days before beggars had learned that his was a household that gave no charity, they'd come to his door by the dozen, asking for food and drink and all the things they were too lazy to earn for themselves. In return, they'd offer to sing the Beggar's Blessing.

The song was an impertinent piece of work. Enhardt already had it running through his head—no, that was from outside. One of his neighbors must have given that woman wine. Or perhaps it was a different beggar singing; no doubt the swarms had begun to descend. Enhardt scowled

---

He cursed his carelessness the moment he opened the door. The man on his front step was not Tschauber. He was a gnarled stick of a man...

---

and hoped none of his neighbors would be too easily fleeced this year. One bit of charity was bad enough, but the more they gave, the more verses the beggar sang. There was one for wine, and another for bread, and cheese, and ale, and apples . . . Enhardt stomped back to his desk, mouth twisted into a grimace. Fools, the lot of them. And now he'd have the song in his head for days.

"Some cheese, if you've got aught to spare
It's noble, sir, for you to share
May you have ten times more next year
So we'll get cheese again from here."

He had scarcely sat down again when the second knock came.

Enhardt's eyes narrowed in annoyance. The woman was persistent, was she? Well, he'd teach her not to come to his door again.

But when he opened the door, a different woman stood there. This one was much older, with her hair thickly graying. She gave him a smile that revealed missing teeth. "Bright the night to you, sir, and may Naus Mannein bring you joy. Have you got cheese to spare for a poor old woman?"

"No, I haven't," Enhardt snapped, glaring at her. The woman's smile faltered. "Go away."

The wind gusted strongly at his words, forcing Enhardt to slit his eyes against the ice crystals it carried. When he looked again, the woman seemed to have shrunk in on herself, huddling against the cold. "Just some ale, then, to warm my blood," she begged. "The night will be bitter hard."

Enhardt almost suggested the beggars all get together and sleep in a heap like dogs to stay warm. But he didn't want to start a conversation; he wanted the woman to go away. "Find some other fool to swindle," he said, and shut the door.

Much of the house's warmth had escaped, and Enhardt's mood darkened as he went back to his chair. He added more wood to the fire before sitting down, but it did little to help. The wind was picking up. It carried the sound of singing to his ears -- a child's voice, whether boy or girl he could not tell, soaring high and pure over the moan of the wind.

"A drop of milk can keep us strong
When winter nights are cold and long
May you have ten times more next year
So we'll get milk again from here."

That voice stayed in Enhardt's mind despite his attempts to get rid of it. He even resorted to humming under his breath, but he could not carry a tune, and outside he could still hear the beggars singing.

But he concentrated on his work, and succeeded in ignoring the noise outside until it was time for Tschauber to come. When the expected knock finally came, Enhardt's mood had improved as much as it could. He rose, added another log to the fire, and went to let the clerk in.

He cursed his carelessness the moment he opened the door. The man on his front step was not Tschauber. He was a gnarled stick of a man, with a face so deeply lined that his eyes peered out as if from two caves. They fixed on Enhardt with disturbing directness, but when the man spoke, his voice was so weak it barely reached Enhardt's ears.

"Milk, or eggs?" the man rasped. "I haven't eaten in three days."

Enhardt ground the words out through clenched teeth. "I don't give charity. Tell all your friends, and tell them to stay away. The next one of you who disturbs me, I shall chase off with a stick."

The man raised shaking hands in entreaty, but Enhardt closed the door on him. He waited a moment, until he heard the old man shuffle off the steps, then went upstairs to his bedroom to fetch a walking stick. Annoyance heated his blood, keeping him warm in the chill air of his chamber. He worked for his living. The cheek of these beggars -- expecting free food and drink in exchange for nothing more than a song -- roused him as little else could. A meaningless blessing of prosperity, for the stores he'd bought with his own money. What did they take him for?

"Good meat puts strength back in our arms
Keeping us alive and warm
May you have ten times more next year
So we'll get meat again from here."

Pounding came from downstairs. Enhardt had gotten warier; he did not head for the door immediately. Instead he went to the room's tiny window and pressed his face up against the icy glass, peering downward to his front step.

The imperfections in the glass made it hard to see, but the figure outside was much too small to be Tschauber. Enhardt squinted, trying to make out details. It looked like the baker's errand boy. Enhardt had thought the new bread wasn't due until tomorrow, but he might have been wrong.

Nevertheless, he kept his walking stick with him as he went downstairs, and put it in front of him as he opened the door a crack and looked out.

It was a boy on his step, all right, but not the baker's apprentice. The lad gave him a brash smile and said, "Bright the night to you! Got any beef to spare?"

"Beef?" Enhardt's mouth fell open at this impudence. "Insolent brat! You think I would spare valuable beef for a street rat like you?"

"Oh, I'm not picky." The boy's grin widened. "Ham would be fine, too. Or hare—I haven't eaten hare in a long time. Even fish, although I'm a bit sick of that."

Enhardt's outrage was such that he didn't even care about the wind blowing into his house, or the snow drifting up against his shoes. "I will not—" he began, but while he was groping for angry enough words, the boy slipped right past him and into the house.

"Hey, nice! Mind if I sit by your fire for a bit? I stopped feeling my toes around mid-afternoon." The boy dropped himself right into Enhardt's own chair before the hearth.

The walking stick clattered to the floor as Enhardt crossed the room in long strides and grabbed the boy by the ear. "Filthy little guttersnipe," he snarled. "How

Shroud #2 March/April

dare you come in here—sit in my chair—I'll set dogs on you! I'll throw you back down into the sewer you came from!" His face heated with fury.

The boy managed to keep talking even as Enhardt dragged him back to the door. "Just give me a couple of apples, then, and I'll be on my way." His breath hissed through his teeth; Enhardt had yanked harder. "Or jellied cranberries. I'm partial to cranberries. Any fruit, really --" and then they were outside, in the ankle-deep snow.

Enhardt shoved him into the deserted street and roared after him, "Don't even think about coming back! I'll beat you to within an inch of your life, you greedy—"

A startled cough brought Enhardt around in the snow. He glared at the muffled figure in front of him before recognizing it as Tschauber, bundled up against the cold. It was only when he saw the clerk that Enhardt realized how bitter the air had grown.

"Is there a problem?" Tschauber asked.

Enhardt did not answer, but stalked back up the steps into his house. A woman approached him from the side, but did not get past "Sir, some vegetables—" before his strides had taken him out of reach. Enhardt waited only long enough for Tschauber to come inside, then slammed the door on the rest of the world.

Tschauber eyed him sideways, but did not say anything. The man knew his job was to keep the accounts, and no more. He sat down in front of the fire and began to spread his papers out, pre-

paratory to making his report.

Even next to the fire, Enhardt felt the cold. And try though he did to focus on Tschauber's words, he could not block out the singing from outside. It sounded like all the beggars in town were out there. He shook his head repeatedly as if that would make the noise stop, and the clerk gave him puzzled looks. Enhardt scowled and told him to get on with his job.

Tschauber went on, but the singing did not stop. It was starting to drive Enhardt mad.

Finally Enhardt slammed one hand onto the table. Tschauber jerked back, words dying on his lips. Enhardt glared at the walls as if he could see the beggars through them. "I can't think with all that damnable noise," he snarled.

"Sir?" Tschauber said.

"The singing, man. The singing! How can you ignore it?" Enhardt stood up; the clerk did likewise, moving more slowly, papers forgotten in his hands. "We will work no more today. Come back next week." He stalked toward the door, leaving Tschauber to gather his things hastily and follow after. "I cannot think," Enhardt repeated, yanking the door open. "Come back when they are gone, when I no longer have to listen to them."

Tschauber stared at him. When Enhardt met his eyes, though, the clerk gave a startled little jump and scurried out into the street, casting one last look over his shoulder before vanishing into the snow-filled twilight.

"We beggars poor ask you for bread
That by your hand we might be fed
May you have ten times more next year
So we'll get bread again from here."

Enhardt shut the door with a bang, but it did not stop the singing. He stood, body tense, hands drifting toward his head, but they could not block the noise. "Silence!" he screamed, shaking with the force of it. "Leave me be!"

He pressed his hands to his ears and squeezed his eyes shut, but the song continued, and then an image came to him.

The street outside, coated in white, pristine and unmarred. Not marked by footprints, or even the tracks of a carriage.

Deserted.

There was no one outside.

Enhardt's eyes shot open. Nonsense; it had to be. He heard the singing. But his mind held that image, of Tschauber hurrying down the street, the only living creature in sight.

Slowly, as if of its own will, his hand crept to the doorknob.

He opened the door and the winter wind came in. Enhardt moved out onto the front step, heedless of the cold. He took one stride, and then another, until he was standing in the middle of the empty street. There was no one there, but the singing went on.

The snow blew into his face, freezing his lips, his ears, coating his eyelashes with ice. Enhardt turned a slow half-circle, eyes passing unheeding over the deserted street, until he was facing his house once more.

The singing stopped.

There was someone on his front step. Enhardt drifted closer, feet shoving through piles of snow. Not one person -- two. The second lay in front of the door, shrunk into a little huddle, scarecrow arms curled tight around his body, a futile defense against the killing cold.

Kneeling over him was the young woman, the first one. Her hazel eyes were bloodshot and stood out terribly in her white, white face.

"Bread," she whispered through lips cracked and bleeding. "Surely you cannot refuse bread. If not for me, then for him."

Enhardt stared down at the dying man. The skull-like face struck him like a blow. Familiar. The beggar man from earlier. Enhardt couldn't remember what he had asked for.

"This is his last chance," the woman said. Her desperate eyes, full of sorrow and warning, held Enhardt frozen. "Your last chance. This could be you. But you still have a choice."

The singing had stopped. As if the voices were waiting, holding their breath.

The cold had penetrated to the marrow of his bones, leaving no warmth in him.

Enhardt stepped past her, over the man's huddled body, and into his house.

He closed the door, but the house was already as cold as a

tomb, and the fire was almost dead. Enhardt passed the hearth without pausing, went to the cellar door, where he lit a candle. This he carried with him down the stairs, to the death-cold room below, where his carefully hoarded food was stored.

Enhardt reached the bottom of the stairs and raised the candle to look around and reassure himself with the sight of the well-stocked room.

It was empty.

He stared, uncomprehending. The bins of fruit and vegetables, the dried meat and fish, the milk and eggs the errand boy had delivered that morning, the wheels of cheese—all gone. He put one hand on a barrel of ale, and it rolled easily at his touch.

Empty.

Only a few crumbs remained on the shelf at his left hand, a mocking reminder of the bread which had been there before he refused the beggars even that.

"This could be you."

Enhardt saw the face of the beggar man from that afternoon as clearly as if he had appeared in the cellar, and it was not the face of the man dying in the snow outside.

His hands rose, shaking, to touch his own face.

The singing had stopped, and would not start again. Inside and out, the air carried frost. Enhardt, alone in his empty cellar, sank to his knees as he felt the first pang of hunger.

◇◇◇◇◇

Marie Brennan's first two novels, **Doppelganger** *and its sequel* **Warrior and Witch,** *came out last year from Warner Books. Next year her third novel,* **Midnight Never Come,** *will be appearing in trade paperback. her short fiction has been published in Dark Wisdom, Talebones, the* **Beneath the Surface** *anthology from Shroud, and the Shadow Box anthology,*

SHROUDED PERSPECTIVES

1968: The Year That Changed Horror
by Peter Gutiérrez

For American society and politics it may have been a heartbreaking, disillusioning year, filled with chaos, bloodshed, and pessimism. But for horror it was arguably the best year ever—perhaps for these very reasons.

For Hollywood's Golden Age, 1939 is often cited as the pinnacle, a year that yielded an almost silly number of classics. Nearly 30 years later, horror had its 1939, producing startling successes on multiple levels and creating an unparalleled watershed for the genre.

Michael Reeves' brilliant *Witchfinder General,* largely vilified at first for its brutality, spurred similarly-themed imitators on the Continent for the next five years. Though made at Tigon, it still represents the apex of Hammer-style British productions—a literate period piece that nonetheless refuses to skimp on the horror. The film also boasts a fine performance by Vincent Price and represents a kind of culmination of the many period films he had done with Roger Corman.

At the same time, as if to prove the ultimate inability of period horror and aging icons to keep pace with the real world, came Peter Bogdanovich's stunning debut, Targets. Not simply the first self-reflective horror movie—a trend that seems to have become a subgenre—Targets also helped bring horror out of the escapist-only mode and deal with true events head-on.

In unintentional contrast to these social statements, one of the world's foremost directors went inward to create one of the most unsettling films ever made. Ingmar Bergman's Hour of the Wolf was a critical hit, but its real legacy was to artists such as David Lynch, who saw new possibilities for using film's unique strengths to replicate internal states experientially for the audience. Anytime you see a film explore madness in a way that undermines reality itself, you might want to thank Bergman.

Until 1968, horror movies had never exactly been nice, but now the genre was becoming subver-

Impact and Influences

I was ten when George A. Romero's Night of the Living Dead was released in October of 1968. That movie did more than just make an impression on a very impressionable kid. In fact it's not an exaggeration to say that movie marked me. It took a bite out of me and I can still feel the scar. I sat in the dark and thought about how overwhelming a rising of the dead would be, and I got really, really scared... and that was wonderful. I remember very clearly sitting in my balcony seat watching that movie and becoming suddenly very aware of how big and dark that balcony was. How far from the lights of the lobby it was. How remote it was. It was like a hand reached into my brain and turned the dial on my imagination up. All the way up. It was at that point that I knew I'd grow up to write horror, which is now my 9-5 job.

—**Jonathan Maberry,** Stoker-winning author of ***Ghost Road Blues*** and the forthcoming ***Zom-***

bie CSU: the Forensics of the Living Dead

Most children are taught to repress their fear of the elderly even as they are being read stories nightly about crones that want to eat them. To me, Rosemary's Baby showed the oldsters as I secretly suspected they were: cult-like and poisoning everyone with their bad-tasting food that was supposed to be good for you. Doctors are shown to not only be full of hot air, but also with their patients' worst interests at heart... [and then there's] the little zombie girl in NOTLD. If you go with the popular idea that the film struck a nerve [related to] the horrors of Vietnam, she seems to represent the next generation that these atrocities were committed in order to protect. Her presence and her eventual "turning" seem to reflect a fear that not only were the next generation not going to toe the line and continue with the status quo, but also that they were more likely to resent their inheritance and shove a gardening tool into their parents' backs as a "Thank you." That's why you still see her image on T-shirts, posters, and postcards—she's actually a symbol of rebellion. Mom and Dad may have done everything to save her, but now she's as out of control as their perceived threat.
—**Lance Vaughan**, critic and co-founder **Kindertrauma.com**

Night of the Living Dead rocked my world—it was so brutal, so real, such an incessant non-stop assault. This was a case where the horror film truly benefited from being ultra low-budget—

sive in ways it rarely had, at least not with such popular success.

Undermining the status quo was certainly what the two undisputed landmark films of 1968 were all about. *Rosemary's Baby* was released on June 12, exactly one week after RFK was shot by Sirhan Sirhan, and four days after James Earl Ray was arrested. These were more than violent times; they were times of upheaval. Just the previous month had seen the Paris student and worker strikes, which led many to believe a full-scale revolution was imminent. It was in this context, which of course dovetailed with several major offensives in the Vietnam War, that Polanski's film soon became a box office and critical hit.

Night of the Living Dead was released in October, barely a month after the rioting at the Democratic National Convention and on the eve of Mexico City's notorious Tlatelolco Massacre of students and workers (ten days before

Original 1968 poster for Romero's *Night of the Living Dead*.

the Olympics). While those familiar with the film's storied history know that ultimately the film grossed tens of millions of dollars on a budget of just over $100K, it was not a real commercial success until the 1969 re-release that followed its acclaim in Europe. And although actually shot in 1967, Night of the Living Dead is very much a 1968 film in spirit. Indeed, Romero and Russell ("Johnny") Streiner drove the finished print to New York to find a distributor on April 4, 1968, the same evening on which Martin Luther King, Jr. was assassinated.

Although these two films have radically different pedigrees and approaches to filmmaking, they share an unsparing nihilistic vision. Neither provided upbeat closure for audiences, and their box office successes forever altered the horror landscape. While other horror films had been downbeat, usually in the classically "tragic" mode, few were so radically pessimistic. Could one get away with that kind of monstrously bleak outlook and still make money? For both major studios and minor independents the answer was a resounding "yes." And of course filmmakers themselves couldn't help but notice the chances these films took—and how such risks paid off.

In short, the American horror film went big-budget and low-budget—and both with such staggering results that producers and distributors could use them as object lessons for years to come. Rosemary's Baby showed Hollywood that money was to be made in A-level adaptations of best-selling novels on contemporary themes, a formula later repeated with The Exorcist and Jaws. Night of the Living Dead, on the other hand, continues to inspire filmmakers working outside Hollywood, and its mythic-vision-on-a-shoestring sensibility represents an important precursor to Halloween a decade later.

So what was it about each of these films that so reflected—and strikingly amplified—the tumultuous times in which they premiered?

Rosemary's Baby, while not as overtly iconoclastic as Night of the Living Dead, is just as devastating and unapologetic. Made for just over $3 million and returning close to five times that much, it was an unqualified blockbuster. And while novelist Ira Levin can no doubt be credited with the pseudo-Gaslight narrative structure that pits a female protagonist against both her husband and accusations of paranoia, those who made the film created a studio horror title unlike any other that had come before. The closest in terms of sheer thematic audacity was probably Psycho (1960), but even there the monster was captured in the end.

A clue that the page has turned in horror history is provided by the first name that appears on screen: William Castle. Although denied the chance to direct Rosemary's Baby, as producer, Castle put together an inspired assemblage of talent. While the picture bears no resemblance to the earlier gimmick-driven films of Castle's career, it does make nods to classic Hollywood in clever ways. The casting of Ralph Bellamy, always the placid butt of Cary Grant's jokes, allowed him to play both with and, eventually, against type. And it is immediately obvious just how desperate Guy Woodhouse is to join the upper middle class when the very first scene has him trying to impress Elisha Cook, Jr.—when had that ever happened in movie history?

Like Romero, Polanski was a Hollywood outsider, a European who had no sentimentality about deconstructing American movies or mores. Marriage, authority, the promise of upward mobility—all of these became targets. In generic terms, what's most striking is Polanski's transposition of an "old dark house" flick into a modern urban environment (something J-Horror would do to great effect 30 years later). With many of the most chilling scenes shot in bright daylight, Polanski visually reinforces that no matter how well Mia Farrow repaints the apartment or redoes her hair, there's no hope of repressing the corruption and sickness that lie under the surface.

Yet the film's lasting achievement is perhaps its celebrated dream sequences—although that term barely does them justice. With elliptical sound, multiple exposures, and surprising yet fluid

> *the handheld black-and-white camerawork and stark, simple lighting made it look and feel like a documentary. Rather than detract from the film, that cost-effective shooting style made the story more believable.*
> —**Richard Gale,** award-winning director of *Criticized*
>
> *Night of the Living Dead is among the best horror films of the 1960's—of all time, in fact—because of its relentlessness, its nightmarish world gone mad, and a whole new portrayal of the zombie, a character previously known only as an object of Haitiian folklore. The Romero zombie was a genuinely frightening creation. In one groundbreaking movie, Romero combined the monster, the dead coming back to life, and cannibalism. Night of the Living Dead ushered in a whole slew of zombie movies, none coming close to the terror of the original.*
> —**Dennis Seuling**, genre historian and critic, **The Villadom Times**

camerawork, we're invited into something more akin to a hypnagogic state—for both protagonist and audience. Blurring the border between internal and external cues in Rosemary's consciousness, Polanski mines a conceit that only cinema can present so effectively. In short, it's not scary dreams that are most dreadful; it's not being able to identify them confidently as dreams. These striking "mindscreen" sequences contain such eerie beauty and power that it's safe to say that a commercial feature had never been so staggeringly subjective and terrifying at the same time. Indeed, Rosemary's cry of "This is no dream, this is really happening!" could have served as the mantra for the master practitioners of modern American horror that followed in '68's wake, and its echoes can still be heard, throbbing dimly, beneath the genre. So while it's facile to note that without Rosemary's Baby there wouldn't have been The Omen (1976), it's also reasonable to suggest that there'd be no A Nightmare on Elm Street (1984) either.

Finally, the most frightening thing about Rosemary's Baby is nothing apparent on the screen; rather, it's the gradual evaporation of all meaningful context, a prospect both existentially and morally apocalyptic. Yes, Rosemary herself undergoes a physical and emotional transformation, but what's truly awful, as with Gregor Samsa, is what this change reveals about the social and values systems in which she'd felt so secure. Ultimately, Polanski's mise-en-scène emphasizes that she's accepting not just the child but the sinister world of which it

John Cassavettes' Rosemary's Baby

is a creation. Although the birth of the title character is what the movie is ostensibly about, the subtext goes straight for an inversion of Christ's admonishment in John 3:1-8 to be born again. The gestation period the movie details is actually Rosemary's own, and it ends with her emerging into a realm of darkness deeper than that of the womb.

So much has been written about Night of the Living Dead that now it's probably impossible to offer a fresh exegesis. Instead, it's worth noting how rapidly it became so overdetermined in its symbolism, providing a blank field upon which one's fears could be projected. If the viewer thought the zombies were U.S. troops, the "consuming" American public, hedonistic hippies—all right, then that's what they were.

NOTLD's status as an overnight archetype makes it no wonder that the film's march into the canon was as relentless as the film itself. It did more than give legitimacy to the low-budget end of horror; it helped fuel critical studies of the genre for years to come. Eventually this trend would trigger an interest in critically reevaluating or "discovering" other drive-in gems such as Carnival of Souls (1962). So as much as NOTLD pointed the way to the future, it also helped horror reaffirm its past. It united high- and low-brows both within and outside of the horror community, and spoke to cineastes generally. That is, when The Texas Chainsaw Massacre (1974) became part of MOMA's permanent collection, Romero's film deserved a tip of the hat.

Like Rosemary's Baby, NOTLD is about metaphysical and social upheaval—or, more precisely, where the two intersect. Horror audiences already knew the dead could come back if revived by a scientist, a vampiric curse, or a voodoo spell. But Romero's zombies were different: they were clearly us... a thematic breakthrough that, 40 years later, still resonates powerfully in such films as 28 Days Later (2002), Shaun of the Dead (2004), and Fido (2006). In terms of horror's central paradigm, NOTLD broke down the barrier that separated the audience from the Other. There had always been a tacit exchange of identification and even sympathy across that membrane, and some filmmakers made it more permeable than others. But in Romero's film for the first time appears the heretical notion that there is no membrane—Either in movies or in life.

It's clear that the zeitgeist in the late '60s made it possible for audiences not only to tolerate such a bleak message, but also ultimately to embrace it. It's fascinating to go back and read the critical response to these films and see how reviewers warmed up to them, as if they were forced overnight to adapt to the public's new diet in popular entertainment or be left behind. In 1967, with its Summer of Love, such shifts would never have occurred; but a year later, society had irrevocably turned some kind of corner. No doubt about it: people were shocked by Night of the Living Dead's lack of survivors and Rosemary's inability to overcome the conspiracy against her (as some ingénue in a standard suspense film might). But they were more receptive to shocks of this magnitude than ever before; the real world had prepared them. Arguably, today's filmmakers and audiences take for granted the freedom to be nihilistically downbeat that these films unintentionally helped champion.

Between them, Romero and Polanski conquered the twin poles of dread: monsters within and without, familiar as neighbors and as new as SF-spawned zombies. Similarly, their two films are prototypical in terms of "quiet horror" and "splatter" and thus cover the genre's full spectrum. But most importantly, one film dealt with birth, the other death, and both seemed to smash the comforting things that Western civilization had been telling us about these topics for centuries. We already knew we weren't safe in the "in-between" zone called life, where wars and killers lurked, but now there was neither initial innocence nor final escape. Instead, the entire plane of human existence was laid savagely bare... and it was into this territory, fresh and terrible, that the horror film rushed headlong—and never looked back.

◇◇◇◇◇◇

Peter Gutierrez has been working professionally in horror and other genres for about fifteen years. He has sold short fiction into Apex Science Fiction & Horror Digest, TQR Stories, Read by Dawn, Rending the Veil, Unicorn 8, and Dark Territories. In comics, Peter's anthology of Japanese ghost stories, **Shi: Kaidan***, was nominated for an Eisner Award. His horror poem, "his face, a rebbutal" was named "Best of Show" for 2006 by the editors of AntiMuse. He writes on film for Withersin magazine, Firefox News, and the UGO Networks as well as teaches film, comics, and media literacy.*

Beneath The Shroud

An Interview with TIM LEBBON

By Paul Kane

Over the last ten years or so, Tim Lebbon has been making a big splash in genre circles – as well as a name for himself with books such as The Nature of Balance, Face, The Everlasting, Dusk and Dawn. Now a New York Times bestselling author, Tim recently sat down with Shroud to answer a few quick questions and to talk about his latest release, A Whisper of Southern Lights….

Paul Kane: What was your first horror story 'Black Heart' about?
Tim Lebbon: A violent racist gets his comeuppance. That was about ten thousand words long. I entered it for a competition when I was 21 and actually got some nice feedback. That was the first time I'd finished writing something and gone to some effort to submit it somewhere. I've still got it somewhere, but it'll never see the light of day.
Paul Kane: Can you remember how you felt when you had your first story accepted in the small presses?
Tim Lebbon: Yep. Delighted. That was *Peeping Tom Magazine*, Stuart Hughes (the editor) called me and asked for a tweak on the story, then said he'd take it. Every time I sell something now I'm really pleased, but when I sold that story 'First Taste' (and yes, I did sell it, and I have the cheque for £2.50 lying around here somewhere, still), I was thrilled beyond words.
Paul Kane: How did your first novel, *Mesmer,* come about and what was the inspiration for it?
Tim Lebbon: The inspiration was a story I read in the press about a housewife in Italy. She was charging people an entrance fee to go into her kitchen, because ghostly images of human faces were appearing on her flagstone floor, then slowly fading away again, like weird water marks staining the stone. Got to admire her commercial mindedness. I thought it was a striking, really disturbing image (not only what was happening, but the idea of visitors paying to be led past and view this phenomenon … just creepy). I incorporated the

image into the *Wall of Souls*, and the rest of the story grew up and outwards from that.
This was my first real novel, at least the first one I'd finished. I'd sold – or had published – about 30 stories in the small press by then, and I felt it was time to make a proper attempt at a novel. It was far from perfect, but I still like the book, and it still gets me some nice response even now, ten years

later. In fact a foreign publisher has just expressed interest, so we'll see.

Paul Kane: What's the story behind the first line changing?

Tim Lebbon: Ahh ... that was Anthony Barker, my publisher at Tanjen. He thought it needed more of a gripping first line, so he came up with that one. Lots of people complimented me on it. Ha!

Paul Kane: How did your first deal with mass market publishers Leisure come about?

Tim Lebbon: After *Mesmer*, I was writing a second novel for Tanjen, *The Nature of Balance*. This was going to be my big British apocalyptic novel, being a lifetime fan of John Wyndham. But the bank pulled the rug from under Tanjen's feet, and I was left with a finished novel without a publisher. I asked my agent to send it to Leisure, and luckily enough Don D'Auria – the editor there – had already read *Mesmer* (encouraged by a great cover quote from Simon Clark). I think that helped a lot in his eventual decision to buy the book. And that just goes to show cover quotes can sell books!

Paul Kane: What was the initial impetus for the *Assassin Series*, and did you have an overall story arc in mind when you started?

Tim Lebbon: Blame Don Koish. When he wanted to start up Necessary Evil Press, he approached me to write his first title, and suggested a sequel to *Mesmer*. I thought on that, decided I wasn't really keen on writing a sequel ... but the character of Temple suddenly seemed like someone I could explore a little more. So I did. It turned out well, and halfway through writing *Dead Man's Hand* I realised this could be a whole series of novellas, featuring Temple as a supernatural assassin, and Gabriel as the (possibly) immortal man cursed to hunt him down through the centuries. The background story arc is developing as I write the novellas, and yes, I do now have a good idea of where it's going. There'll be at least several more novellas until it's all over.

Paul Kane: The characters of Gabriel and Temple appear to represent good and evil at a fundamental level. Would you go along with this?

Tim Lebbon: I've never been comfortable with the concept of pure good and pure evil, not in real life or in fiction. Sure, Temple is a bit of a bastard, but he has a humour that Gabriel does not, and perhaps there are revelations to come that will turn his character around. Who knows? And Gabriel, the hunter, is doing so selfishly – revenge for his dead family. He doesn't really care who gets hurt along the way.

Paul Kane: And Gabriel seems to get the roughest deal in all of these, doesn't he?

Tim Lebbon: Most of the time, yeah. He's like Ash in Evil Dead. There's a reason for this, of course. But if I told you I'd have to kill you.

Paul Kane: You've used historical settings such as the Old West, pirate times, and now WWII – did you have to do a lot of research for the novellas?

Tim Lebbon: More than for anything else I've ever written. But the research is a lot of fun, and I enjoy it ... it's quite refreshing, actually, as when I'm writing *Noreela* stories (my fantasy world), everything is made up. The only research I have to do is reading my own work, making sure timelines and geographies match up, that sort of thing. Writing the *Assassin Series* is great, because I get to read about some wonderful, scary and dreadful times and places. And I'm writing about times and places that interest me anyway, so the research reading really doesn't feel like a chore.

Paul Kane: You've said that the last line of *A Whisper of Southern Lights* has caused quite a stir – can you say anything more about what might be ahead for the series?

Tim Lebbon: The last two lines of *Whisper* will give the reader a hint of where this is going, but not how we'll get there, nor what will happen when we arrive. And like I said, I've got a good idea of the future, but it's not all planned out in detail. I hate planning.

Paul Kane: What's coming up in the immediate future from you that we should be looking out for?

Tim Lebbon: After the *War* is out now from Subterranean Press. *A Whisper of Southern Lights* will be out soon from Necessary Evil Press. In April, Bantam will publish the next Noreela novel *Fallen*, then in May they'll release *Mind the Gap*, the first of a novel series

I'm writing with Chris Golden. *Children of the New Disorder* is a novella I co-wrote with Lindy Moore (pseudonym of a popular children's writer), and Creeping Hemlock Press will publish that soon. Sometime this year there'll also be a massive new collection of short fiction, a short novel and a co-edited anthology, though none of these are officially announced. And there's another deal I'm itching to spill the beans on, but I can't just yet. Of course, keep an eye on www.timlebbon.net and there'll be loads more news. Who needs sleep?

◇◇◇◇◇

Paul Kane's genre journalism has appeared in magazines like Fangoria, SFX and Rue Morgue, and he is the author of **The Hellraiser Films and Their Legacy.** *His short stories have been collected in Alone (In the Dark), Touching the Flame and FunnyBones, and his novellas include* **Signs of Life** *(shortlisted for the British Fantasy Awards 2006) and* **The Lazarus Condition** *(introduced by Mick Garris, creator of Masters of Horror). Paul's website, which has featured guest writers such as Stephen King, Neil Gaiman and Clive Barker, can be found at www.shadow-writer.co.uk*

Tim Lebbon's *A Whisper of Southern Lights*
A review by Paul Kane

Necessary Evil Press. 450 Limited numbered softcovers signed by Tim Lebbon, $14. 26 Lettered deluxe hardcovers with a metal traycase signed by Tim Lebbon, Gary A. Braunbeck, and Caniglia ($175). www.necessaryevilpress.com

Tim Lebbon is a name with which every self-respecting horror literature fan should be familiar. Over the years, he's steadily been making a name for himself and building a small army of fans on both sides of the Atlantic. His efforts have garnered a mass market deal with Leisure for books like *The Everlasting*, another with Bantam for his fantasy books *Dusk and Dawn*, and a New York Times bestseller listing just recently for his novelisation of the hit movie *30 Days of Night*.

But Lebbon hasn't forgotten his roots, something that has always endeared him to readers, and with *A Whisper of Southern Lights*, he returns to the small press to continue the story he set in motion with the novellas *Dead Man's Hand* and *Pieces of Hate*. If you're new to the ongoing saga of Gabriel and the demon Temple (also known as The Twin), locked in a cat and mouse game through the centuries, then you've missed out. Fortunately, this third installment can also be enjoyed as a standalone because Lebbon brings the reader up to speed quickly and effortlessly: Gabriel still pines for his murdered family, and is soon set on his quest by the "Man with the Snake in his Eye."

Set this time during World War II, as the Japanese are taking over Singapore, we find Gabriel a battered soul – mentally and physically. As he muses to himself, where is he to start looking for shapeshifting Temple, when there is so much murder and mayhem already happening all around? The answer comes when Temple goes after a soldier called Jack Sykes, who was told a terrible secret by a dying comrade in the jungle, and is now a prisoner in Changi Jail. The one-eyed Gabriel determines to find Sykes before Temple can kill him. If they can escape from the jail, they might both be able to uncover the mystery of what happened back in the jungle. But Temple is on their trail; the revelation that comes at the end will change things forever, and prove just why their battle is so important.

Told in both first and third person (a method also used to great effect by Michael Marshall in his Straw Men trilogy), Lebbon is able to switch between Gabriel's story, told from an observer's point of view, and Sykes' mind as he struggles to come to terms with what is happening. The overall story arc is epic, and yet Lebbon doesn't forget the little details, the nuances. His descriptions, as usual, are first rate (one in particular of a war-torn Singapore street will stay with you forever). Like Gary A. Braunbeck in his introduction (who reminds us that Temple was first seen way back in Mesmer), I can't recommend this one highly enough. Roll on Book 4 in the Assassin Series!

"Haven" by Emily Tolson

HAVEN
Kealan Patrick Burke
(Illustrated by Emily Tolson)

"It's your mother. I'm afraid she's passed away."

Yes, yes. Old news. Never once has he stopped to think about how odd it is that he is so certain. The knowledge was just there, shortly before the phone rang, manifesting itself as an ability to breathe unrestricted, to straighten his shoulders and not meet the resistance of her eternal gaze, to dust off a genuine smile and use it without feeling it ephemeral.

Gone, and the days that follow are among the most wonderful he's ever had. Scarcely had he dared to imagine the release could be so full, so overwhelming, allowing him to tread with lightened step and floating heart. He encounters strangers, and rather than showing them the top of his head in a cowl of cowardice and shame, he beams at them and bids them the sentiments in accordance with the age of the day. That these greetings are seldom reciprocated bothers him little, for his resolve is growing ever more formidable now that he has only one shadow trailing behind him.

Gone, and the nights exude peace, the mattress accepting his tired bones like clay in the hands of a potter. His dreams are golden, exorcised of the heavy cloying darkness that was the signature of life with Mother. There is no doubt that he loved her, but she molded him into a creature of indifference, isolating him in his own little box of shadow where there was never room for any kind of feeling.

He suspects what little grief he feels at her passing stems from his being accustomed to her constant presence, rather than any true emotion. This suspicion in turn ignites guilt, but guilt is something he has learned to master and, aided by his newfound happiness, is soon beaten into submission.

The celebration of her death is a tawdry affair, and Tom finds himself at the hub of a ring of people he doesn't know--nor does he care to. The minister is a patrician man at least twenty years his senior, all practiced smiles and Bible passages as he leads them in a chorus of emotionless verse that rises like startled ravens above the gloomy fall graveyard. The air smells of cold earth and dying leaves.

Tom weathers the condolences, secretly wondering what it is about death that leads people to the assumption that they can immediately insinuate themselves into the lives of the grieving. If anything, he finds a note of condescension in those voices, powered by the look of there but for the grace of God in their eyes. It sickens him and reinforces his need to leave as soon as this stunted procession of sympathy is over.

When the last bleak face has moved away, he stuffs his hands into the pockets of his dark overcoat and rounds the church, the sympathizer's last words to him carried on ill-formed tendrils of autumn wind, falling just short of his desire to hear them.

Grumbling, he slips through the wrought-iron church gate, the spire of St. Andrew's like a chiding finger at his back, reminding him who might be watching his disregard for all things sacred. The image weighs on his shoulders like the memory of the woman he has left behind him in the ground. A woman he scarcely knows.

***

He has come home to the house on Marrow Lane.

As expected, his mother complains about the length of his hair, how much weight he has lost. She asks him why he has bothered to come visit her after so long an absence. Her frequent wincing and moaning about her incessant headaches render his excuses meaningless.

"They steal my sleep, and it's getting harder to keep anything down."

"You need to eat to keep your strength up," he replies, feeling achingly redundant and thinking: Who is this woman?

Her dramatics are almost certainly a cry for attention, a trait not unknown to her and worsened by age. He delivers the customary platitudes and takes his leave of her, ushered out on a cloud of protest only silenced by the thick oak door of the house.

***

Now, standing before that very same door, running a trimmed fingernail over the cracks and ridges in the wood grain, he ponders the irony of her death.

An aneurysm. If it's any consolation, I doubt she felt a thing. It would have been very sudden.

I see.

Had she been complaining about headaches or dizziness lately?

No. At least, not to me...

Realizing he might have been able to save her had he taken her histrionics seriously brings to mind a far darker question: Had you known, would you have done anything?

Brushing the thought aside, he opens the door of the two-story memory vault he used to call home. As he steps into the hall, his senses hone in on the smallest, the slightest (Tommy, is that you?) of sounds. He waits, the dust settling around him in the chorus of quiet, ears attuned to the soundtrack of the old house. Eventually he straightens, exhales heavily, and continues down the hall until he comes to the living room.

From the doorway, he sees the familiar sight of the old 10" television set in the opposite corner. A miniscule and fog-shrouded representation of himself is all that shows on the vapid eye of the screen as he enters the room.

The beige carpet knots itself beneath his shoes, and he resolves to have it torn up as soon as he moves in proper. He suspects that foul, vomit-colored layer of shag is older than himself, and he has hated it for as long as he can remember.

The same goes for the sofa, a bloated brown semblance of intestines passing itself off as Naugahyde. The upholstery is ripped, yellow foam winking lewdly at him from elliptical eye-sockets. Gone, he thinks, relishing the thought of being rid of these particular harbingers of memory. His double shadow bids him look up, and he nods at the imitation gold chandelier, missing two of its four bulbs, then down to the once white wallpaper, curling from the mildewed plaster beneath...Gone.

The photographs, sepia and black-and-white depictions of stern-faced young men cradling even sterner looking women in their burly arms, people he has never met but who he assumes are his relatives...Gone.

Gone, gone, gone. All of it. Anything not immediately pertaining to his life will be dumped with an abandon impervious to the wheedling pleas of sentimentality. It is, after all, his castle now.

Grinning, he makes his way down the hall to the kitchen. This room seems smaller than he remembers it, and he wonders if it has shrunk in on itself after years of absorbing the auras of subconscious misery from the inhabitants of this place.

The lemon-hued walls seem to sag as he wanders around the room. He sniffs at the leaky radiator with the small plastic bowl beneath the tap to catch the water and shakes his head at the grease-smeared range, the picture on the wall above it speckled with spots so that the faces of the two watercolor children look positively leprous. A foul smell drifts to his nose from the trash compactor beneath the sink. He decides to investigate that some other time.

Against the far wall stands a simple pine table with three chairs, and it is here his gaze stalls as the bloated corpse of memory rises to the surface of his mind.

You're a dreamer, Tommy, you'll always be a dreamer, and a man who spends too much time in his own head never gets a goddamn thing done.

Don't talk to him like that.

I don't remember anyone asking you're opinion, Agnes. It's a sweet life for both of you, living in your daydreams while I'm out busting my ass to put food on the table.

Tom stems the flow of recollection, feels it swell against his resistance. The surface of the table is pitted with scratch marks and tiny holes where knives have been used to make a point. Coffee rings on the left—his mother's side of the table—stare up at him like blinded eyes. On the right, paler circles where his father lost himself in the liquid utopia of liquor.

And in the middle where Tom used to sit, there is nothing.

He can almost see himself now—a young boy, eyes permanently narrowed in anticipation of a blow that could come at any time, skin sallow, devoid of the youthful glow typical of a child his age, sitting in a chair that only emphasizes his diminutive frame, his parents flanking him like birds of prey, always watching and waiting as if they expect something profound to trickle from his small tight-lipped mouth. But Tommy remains silent as much as possible. It is safer.

Shrugging off the memory, Tom shuffles over to the range and the bulbous white kettle, the base blackened by time and negligence, the handle loose, screws rattling. He opens it and angles it toward the naked bulb behind him. To his surprise it appears moderately clean. Nevertheless, he rinses it until he is sure nothing untoward will end up in his cup, fills it and lights the gas ring beneath. The thought of piping hot coffee staves off the unpleasant chill which reminiscence has brought in tow.

Suddenly the blue flame beneath the kettle sputters as the kitchen door drifts open. He turns as it groans wide, allowing him to see down the length of the hallway.

Damn it.

The front door is standing open. He figures he must have forgotten to close it when he came in, so drawn was he by the familiar. He stomps down the hall, grabs the door handle, and is pushing it closed when a faint shuffling gives him pause. He listens, glances at his wristwatch: almost eight. Not an odd time for people to be out wandering, surely?

Peering around the edge of the door and out onto the cracked pavement reveals nothing except the lazy onset of twilight; the air is heavy, and stars twitch into life in the vermilion canvas that hangs above Marrow Lane. A neighborhood dog yaps and growls, yips and whines like a violin with ill-tuned strings. Someone yells: "Shut that damn dog the hell up," and is ignored.

Tom frowns and shivers at the autumn chill insinuating its way through the fabric of his coat. Just as he is about to shut the door, he catches sight of an old woman standing by the streetlight a few feet down from his house, her hair a wild halo of sodium fire. She is dressed in nothing more than a housecoat and slippers, and appears to be staring right at him, sending an unwelcome spark of unease through him. He backs away from the door, starts to ease it closed.

The old lady moves.

He pauses, one eye peeking through the inch-wide space between door and jamb, watching, though now he feels as if he has donned a coat of snakes. His skin crawls as the shadow-faced woman moves along the sidewalk with short, stiff steps, the orb of fuzzy darkness hiding eyes that may or may not be fixed on him. She shuffles closer still and he realizes this is the sound he heard earlier. Shhhnick! Shhhnick! Shhhnick!

He wants to close the door, an action that will leave his sudden inexplicable fear outside with the old woman, but he is powerless to do anything but watch.

She reaches the mailbox—a simple black tin semi-cylinder staked in Tom's garden but jutting out over the pavement—and stops, cocks her head and brings a gnarled hand toward it.

Is she pilfering the mail or what? he wonders, his unease no less potent as he rapidly abandons the idea of confronting her.

He hears the soft scraping sound of the mailbox door opening, and watches in disbelief as the old lady stoops down and peers inside. After a moment in which he imagines he can feel the victory radiating in icy waves from her skeletal frame, her hand emerges holding a small white rectangle. Clutching the letter to her chest, she swivels on her heels and shuffles back up the street, passing through the orange glow from the streetlight much more quickly than she had on her way to steal the mail.

I should have done something. He watches the shadows swallow her. That letter might have been important.

The kettle shrieks and jars the thought from his head.

***

Later that evening, he stands at the threshold to a time capsule, held in place by a feeling of unreality that almost makes him dizzy.

Over the last few years, his visits to this house have been infrequent. and he has never stayed. In fact, he came armed with a plethora of excuses should such a thing be suggested. As a result, he has never come upstairs and seen his old room.

He is shocked to find it is exactly the same, from the crimson toy chest at the foot of the bed to the Mickey Mouse wallpaper. His old teddy bear Rufus, now missing an eye, sits atop a once white pillow, arms splayed in frozen greeting. The carpet whispers as he advances further into the sanctuary of his childhood, head pounding, eyes wide with the strain of trying to absorb the sudden rush of familiarity.

A small oak desk, rescued from the local dump and restored to nothing like its former glory by Tom's father in one of his rare charitable moods, stands solemnly before the small white-framed arched window overlooking the neighboring rooftops.

Through one of the four panes, a thin crack like mercury lightning streaks an eternal path in the glass from top to bottom. Beyond that, the darkness rolls over the silent neighborhood, dampening the sounds of life and nodding its ethereal assent to the night creatures and the hunters waiting for their time to shine.

Tom shakes his head, looks down at the pockmarked surface of the desk and remembers... Just as his father jabs the kitchen table with his knife or fork or the stub of his carpenter's pencil, so Tommy waits until he is alone and punctuates his own confused anger with the corner of a ruler, or pen, or…

"Did I hate him?" Tom asks the empty room. "Did I hate them both and not know it?"

He kneels before the desk as if it is the armrest in a confessional. His knees quickly grow sore on the threadbare carpet. He studies the indecipherable doodles and unfinished scribbles printed on the table. Only one is clear and etched with an angry hand into the wood:

HAVEN

This one he understands, even if he can't quite remember carving it.

In here, in this room, he had been permitted to believe the misery wasn't endless, that someday his father would arrive home wearing a smile in place of his ever-present scowl, smelling of wood and sawdust instead of whiskey. In here, solitude had provided the perfect movie screen for the illusions his hope projected, and as long as he stayed here, nothing could break the spell which imagination wove around him. Here were peace, love, and happiness. Out there, over the moat and a million miles away, were misery, hate, and pain.

Tom lifts his head and looks out at the encroaching darkness unique to the season. He pictures the dying leaves caught in a maelstrom, spinning around in a mindless vortex like lost souls, and he realizes nothing has changed.

As he gets to his feet, he sees himself again, youthful body hunched over the desk, hiding the bruises on his face, weeping as he mourns the death of another fantasy at the vicious hands of reality.

He decides then that he will not stay here tonight. Even though he has long since dismissed the idea that adolescent fantasies can soften the edges of life, he doesn't want to sleep in a place where that very belief died.

This room is haunted, but not by ghosts. He can sense his childhood self here, the child that has stayed in this room, poring over the marks on the table, still hating the Mickey Mouse wallpaper, still trying to figure out why his daddy beats him while his mother watches with tears in her eyes. He is still angry and probably still dreaming of a better life he will never get.

"But my life did get better,"

Tom tells the silent room, surprised by the lack of conviction in his voice. The taste of stale coffee clings to the back of his throat as he swallows and turns to leave. *Stop lying to yourself. This was the only safe place.*

The voice in his head is devoid of malice but filled with determination. He ignores it, for it is just another unwanted memory, one he has the luxury of dismissing.

With a rattling sigh, he slowly makes his way back downstairs. He wonders if it might be better to put the house up for sale, to let someone oblivious to the horrid memories make it their home, someone immune to the tapestries of pain fashioned from the dust itself and the sting of sharp tongues still lingering in the air.

He thought it would be different coming back here, that his mother had been the only remaining anchor to a past too dreadful to contemplate. A foolish assumption. If anything, her presence had allowed him to think only of her part in the shadow play that had been his childhood. With her gone, the curtains were thrust open, every room a set upon which the dramas of a miserable youth waited for an audience.

But the fact remains that he has no place else to go.

He supposes a few weeks here won't hurt, just until he comes up with something better. Perhaps an extended vacation, to clear his head and relax for the first time in as long as he can remember.

He stops at the bottom of the stairs, sure he hasn't heard what his brain is telling him he has. A few moments of listening yield nothing to confirm there has been any noise, and the tension begins to ebb from his muscles.

Then it comes, softly, seeping under the door like floodwater: *Shhhnick! Shhhnick! Shhhnick!* He doesn't move; waits instead for what he is now certain will follow.

A brief scratching like nails on a garage door.

Or an old mailbox being opened.

This is crazy.

It takes a great deal of effort for him to swallow the knot of inexplicable fear that has lodged in his throat, but he is suddenly tired of being afraid, can't remember the last time he hasn't been, and a surge of uncharacteristic resolve brings him to the door, makes him wrench it open, propels him down the garden path and delivers him to the mailbox and the old lady standing before it.

She is peering once again into the bulbous darkness inside.

"Excuse me," he says, his voice brittle in the cool air.

She ignores him, apparently too intent on her felonious task, but this close he can see that she is a lot older than he first thought; the myriad lines in her sallow face retain the shadows as if they are an intrinsic part of her. The black pools of her eyes are curved at the behest of a toothless smile as she retrieves her second prize of the night from his mailbox.

It occurs to him that he has seen her somewhere before, but is not altogether surprised. Marrow Lane is a small neighborhood.

"Excuse me, but what do you think you're doing?" He wants to tap her on the shoulder, to grab her elbow or anything that might bring her focus round to him, but for some reason he senses that touching her would be a dreadful mistake.

She is holding the small white envelope up to the streetlight, and he has almost conceded--is in fact formulating a parting caveat—when she suddenly turns and says: "You always had a great imagination, Tommy." Then she once again shuffles off into the shadows, leaving him helpless to do anything but watch.

"Wait, who are you?" he cries after her, and she looks back over her shoulder at him, her face a creamy blur in the darkness. Then even the shuffling ceases, and the sounds of night rush back in.

Only the soughing of the wind answers him.

Frowning, he goes back inside.

How did she know my name?

***

In the hallway, Rufus sits against the wall.

Tom stands paralyzed as the door clicks shut behind him, muting the wind.

"Hello?" he asks the hallway, and thinks that if the teddy bear turns his head in response, he will most certainly drop dead of a heart attack. While the old lady was bizarre, she certainly wasn't beyond rational explanation. This, however, is dancing on the boundaries of sanity.

He clearly remembers seeing the toy seated on the bed in his old room. He hadn't moved it, would recall if he had. How then, has it ended up down here?

Horrible images of the teddy bear carefully navigating the stairs while he was outside flash behind his eyes, and he scoffs a little too casually even as he feels his hackles rise.

"To hell with it." He rushes forward and scoops up the stuffed toy, then marches up the stairs, the loud clumping of his boots deliberate and reassuring. If someone else is here, they will know he is coming and that he isn't happy.

He reaches the landing and takes a deep breath, steels himself for whatever he might find in his old bedroom. With his heart chiseling its way through his ribcage, he stalks into the room. And comes to a dead halt.

A little boy, sallow-faced and sheet-white, has replaced Rufus on the bed. An ugly bruise purples his left eye and most of his cheek. He is dressed in Mickey Mouse pajamas, Tom's old pajamas, and as Tom watches, the boy raises his hands to receive the bear. Despite the surrealistic feel reality has draped over its shoulders, Tom tosses the bear to the child and tells himself to remain calm.

"Who are you?"

The boy looks at the bear as if he's addressing not Tom, but the toy. "You know who I am. Who do I remind you of?"

In truth, this is a question Tom has been hoping the boy wouldn't ask, because the answer is something he is not prepared to face. He says: "I don't know."

The child looks amused, and Tom feels his nerves fraying at the edges, unraveling. "How did you get in here?" he asks.

"I'm the one who makes stuff up, not you. So stop pretending you don't already know these things you're asking me."

To accept what is presenting itself as the truth, as reality, as normality, is opening Tom's door wide to insanity. So for now, he will keep on pretending that the child sitting on the bed is not a younger version of himself. He carefully makes his way over to the desk and sits down, his finger absently tracing the striations in the surface of the table that form the word: *HAVEN*.

"I couldn't do it, you know," the boy says, fingering Rufus's eye. "I couldn't bring her back."

"Who?"

"Mom. I guess I thought I'd be able to. After all, I was able to make Gramma come back."

Tom feels his skin grow cold as the old lady at the mailbox flashes before his eyes. She had seemed familiar. Now he knows why, and it brings to mind the sepia-toned pictures of smiling strangers down in the living room.

Without thinking, he blurts: "But she isn't dead. She's in a home in Harperville."

The boy nods. "She found her own safe place. I brought her back here where she belongs, though, just like I thought I could bring Mommy home. Just like I brought you home."

Tom rubs a hand over his face and leans forward. "And who do you think I am?"

"Still pretending you don't know? You're me, the part of me that went on and left me behind, the part of me forced to leave the safe place. You're what escaped." Tom chuckles at that, but it is a sound so far from mirth it frightens him, and his face draws tight with worry. "This is madness. You do see that, don't you? This is like a literal translation of what shrinks mean when they talk about people talking to themselves. I'm expecting to wake any moment in an asylum."

The boy looks at him, his coral blue eyes glistening. "You've often thought there was something missing in your life, haven't you?"

Tom says nothing.

"So have I." For the moment, the stuffed toy is forgotten. "I thought in here nothing could touch me, and for a while it worked. I got to stay where it was safe while you carried on living in the real world, forgetting the make-believe and acting like everyone else. I tried to bring Mommy back when she died, but it didn't work. Gramma came back and you came back, even though you still won't believe."

"What do you want from me?" Tom asks in a voice little more than a whisper.

The child looks back to the toy. "My safe place is crumbling.

I can't be here on my own any more."

"Why? If you've been here this long…" What the hell am I saying? Am I actually buying this? But what the child says next dismisses all doubts, because in the instant the words reach him, he is once more afraid with a fear that transcends all others.

"Daddy came back."

It is irrational, but by now Tom is coming to expect nothing less. He gets to his feet and looks down at the boy, at the fear etched on his face, a terror so suddenly familiar and personal that he believes everything without question, simple as that. Denying this reality any longer will drive him mad.

"He hurt you?"

The child nods. "He slipped through once, when I fell asleep and forgot to close the door all the way. I woke up and saw him standing over me, just a large shadow with gleaming white teeth. Now I keep the door closed." He looks toward the door and Tom follows his gaze.

"Will you stay with me?"

"I don't know." His eyes are fixed on the door. It's open just a crack, but that crack is now as deadly as a yawning abyss.

"There is nothing out there for you. You know that. You've felt it ever since you left."

Tom mutters agreement, but can't look away from the door-- or the shadows crawling up the walls of the stairs beyond.

"Please."

He thinks of the word scratched into the desk, the word he carved there all those years ago when he believed it to be true. Now he realizes it still can be.

Three paces and he is across the room and slamming the door closed.

The boy looks at him and smiles. "We might not be able to keep him out forever."

Tom walks to the bed and sits just below the boy's slippered feet. "We'll see."

His eyes are on the door.

"I missed you," says the boy.

Tom tries to ignore the creaking of the stairs.

∞∞∞∞

Born and raised in Dungarvan, Ireland, Kealan Patrick Burke is an award-winning author described by Publishers Weekly as "a newcomer worth watching" and by Booklist as "one of the most clever and original talents in contemporary horror."

Some of his works include the novels **Currency of Souls, Master of the Moors, Kin, and The Hides** *(Bram Stoker Award nominee, 2005), the novellas* **The Turtle Boy** *(Bram Stoker Award Winner, 2004),* **Midlisters, and Vessels** *(Bloodletting Press), and the collections Ravenous Ghosts (Delirium Books), and The Number 121 to Pennsylvania & Others.*

He has also sold short fiction to Cemetery Dance, Grave Tales, Shivers II, Shivers III, Shivers IV, Looking Glass, Masques V, Subterranean #1, Evermore, Inhuman, Gothic.net, Surreal Magazine, Corpse Blossoms and Postscripts.

You can learn more about Kealan at his website: www.kealanpatrickburke.com.

Shroud #2 March/April

Pink Elephant

By Nathaniel Lambert

Uncle Conrad passed on an uneventful Sunday afternoon. Sometime around the six o'clock news, gauging by the fact that the rest of the family had not yet sat down for the season finale of POLITICAL BATTLE ROYALE—The Reverend Al Sharpton pitted against Ann Coulter and her legion of undead.

What he mistook for mere indigestion, as a consequence of firehouse chili, turned out to be the final leak in the dike. His aorta hit oil big time: blebbed out like a bullfrog's throat and ruptured. While the thoracic cavity flooded with detoured red stuff, his niece's family argued about going over their allotted cell phone minutes. Right around the time his tongue swelled up in a permanent raspberry, the topic shifted to: Why can't a fifteen year old get breast augmentation? All through the death process everyone else made sure they were completely oblivious to poor old Uncle Conrad. The way a ring of white spittle had dried up around his carp lips, and the donut swelling in his neck made him look like "Pogo the Clown."

Right before the end, Uncle Conrad arched his back in some kind of awkward fat man's yoga pose and then fell back down to the chair.

His last moments on earth were met with eye-rolls and puffs of

exasperation. What a taxing old man.

Fortunately, the living room offered ample seating besides Uncle Conrad's favorite recliner: the one that smelled of stale farts and twenty years of Preparation H. The only interruption of the night was when a large amount of malodorous fluid expressed itself with a splatter from the dead uncle's bunghole. That took place during an infomercial for fast acting upholstery cleaner. The niece ordered four bottles.

Moral obligation dictates that if a loved one expires in the family den, it's up to the next of kin to ensure that proper arrangements are in place to ease said loved one's transition into the afterlife. However, Uncle Conrad's family only felt an obligation to themselves. What would they do without his pension to supplement their already titanic monthly expenses? They'd lose everything. There was only one logical answer.

The plan was to feign ignorance. Act as though he were still a thriving member of the family. Call his name for dinner. Make the kids shout a boisterous hello when they got home from school. The husband could talk about the big game on Sunday. Mom could tell Uncle Conrad that Cousin So-and-So sent her love. Keep up appearances until they could find his loot. Rumor had it that Uncle Conrad confiscated a rather large collection of jewelry and gold—some in the form of fillings—during WWII. He was always flapping away that it was stashed somewhere in the house.

***

Throw a sheet over him, fill up all the outlets with scented oils, move the TV into the kitchen, and you'd hardly know there's a dead guy in the house. When friends come over, blanket the whole den in sheets and tell them you're painting. Blame the smell on a backed up sewer pipe next door. When they ask what color you picked, all you can picture is the hue of the fluid that came out of Uncle Conrad.

If they ask where's Uncle Conrad, tell them he's at the VFW for a fish fry.

Call in sick, make the kids stay home, close all the shades and tear the house apart. Start upstairs in the attic with all the memorabilia. Dump out the old suitcases of photographs and film reel. Trample the pictures of Uncle Conrad in uniform or down on one knee proposing. Rip the backs off of the oil paintings and shatter the matting. Knee high in scattered memories. Nothing—fruitless. Move to the downstairs and repeat.

Topple over all the furniture in Uncle Conrad's room. Plug your nose from the overpowering musk from his broken bottles of cat-piss aftershave.

When there's nowhere left to look, no mnemonic stone unturned, collapse in the middle of all the squalor and weep. Your fingernails are cracked and bleeding from digging through the sheetrock. Listen as the answering machine picks up. It's the bank. The signatures didn't match on Uncle Conrad's last check.

***

After three stifling weeks, the stench was unbearable. Hordes of flies hovered above the fetid recliner. They lit down and drank their fill of Uncle Conrad's liquefied tissue right through the sheet, did their mid-flight fucking on top of broken slivers of china, and laid countless eggs in the Berber carpet. When globs of necrotic tissue started sloughing off onto his padded slippers, and the French bulldog gobbled it up like kibble, it was time to move the family into the detached garage.

***

Bill collectors are heartless, apathetic monsters. They don't sympathize with a person who can't go to work because they stink like death. The stuff that wafts off the murky pool of gunk that used to be Uncle Conrad clings to every surface in the house, including bare skin. Wash all you want: that aromatic tattoo is permanent.

All that's left, before the authorities blast through the front door, is to pack everyone up in the leased SUV and slip away to Aunt Patricia's place in Quebec. Make quick work of what's left of Uncle Conrad, and then drive the whole way with all the windows down to let in some fresh air.

***

"Wow, you really fixed this place up. It was a real dump."
"Yeah, I'm going to make a killing off of this flip."

"When I first saw the pictures of the inside, I thought you made a big mistake. It looked like a landfill."

"You'd be surprised by how many overextended families just up and leave everything behind."

"I can imagine."

"The best part is I found a small fortune in jewelry and gold tucked up inside an old rotten chair."

"You lucky bastard."

∞◇◇◇∞

Mad Scientist by day, greenhorn writer by night. Nathan's flash piece "Memory Cell" can be found at www.microhorror.com. The January issue of The Open Vein will feature his story "Out to Pasture". Three of his flash fiction pieces can be found in the up and coming anthology The Twisted Twins—Daily Chills Calender.

Shroud #2 March/April

Your Horror Collection Would be in Ruins without Shroud.

Visit Us Today

www.shroudmagazine.com

Books, Magazines, More

HOME
MAURA MCHUGH

On a moonless night in 1678, Lord Alexander Fitzhugh laid my foundations. Aided by his architect, Francesco Alberti, Alexander sacrificed a badger, a raven, a deer, and a swan. The animals protested their slaughter with fierce cries, but Alexander's hands were steady, brutal. Blood steamed and splashed over my heartstone, pooled in the carved alchemical sigils, and I suckled its quintessence with a newborn's urgent need.

Afterwards, the men sank the carcasses deep in the Hibernian soil beneath the seal of my stone, and chanted ancient spells as a lullaby.

Dirt blanketed me, roots embraced me, and worms laced between teeth bared in anguish. My pulse quickened with love.

***

This is what I gleaned during my construction:

For his Grand Tour, Alexander travelled throughout Europe, buoyed by the funds of his ailing, indulgent father. He scoured libraries and universities, and employed rare book collectors in Paris, Cologne, and Madrid to gather texts on arcane sciences, architecture, and sacred geometry. His agents acquired a copy of Agrippa's Fifth Book of Occult Philosophy, which many sages insisted did not exist in any form in this world. Alexander's research was informed by his study of mathematics, alchemy, and astrology; Newton had tutored him at Cambridge.

With money and the right letters of introduction, Alexander procured initiation with the Fraternity of the Rosy Cross. It admitted him to the association of students of the Invisible College, and via the brotherhood he discovered Francesco in a mouldering athenaeum in Rome. An ignored but clever journeyman of a famous architect, Francesco required little enticement to purloin secrets, abandon his master, and take service with the ambitious Englishman.

Alexander's father, the Viscount Fitzhugh, had never travelled to the sodden and savage lands of Ireland--not with his gout--but his agents gathered coin from the peasants he'd inherited with his title. Alexander decided that such a place, with its wild and romantic landscape, would be the perfect location to raise a citadel of civilisation, a bulwark against barbarian ignorance, and whose very design would furnish him with the key to the secrets of creation.

Thus, Alexander selected my birthplace.

***

The Golden Ratio guided my design, and the Tree of Life dictated the number of my rooms and the flow of paths between them. My walls were built of red bricks fired in Dublin, and smooth

Portland stone--ferried from Dorset--covered my exterior façade. Expert stonemasons followed Francesco's plans with precision, but bemoaned Alexander's strict supervision and the exactitude of his demands.

A phalanx of carpenters carved and fitted hardwoods from the Americas to fashion my sweeping central staircase. My floorboards were hewn from local oak, except for the first floor, which was composed of slabs of Penteli marble--the building blocks of the Acropolis. Italian artists lay on scaffolds and painted frescos on the vaulted ceilings. French designers haggled over gilt furniture for my interiors, and complained about the food and abominable weather. Silks from China and carpets from Morocco adorned my surfaces. Troops of gardeners shaped a symmetrical garden designed upon the principles of harmonious proportion.

I grew and flourished under their care and attention.

Alexander poured a sizeable portion of his fortune into my construction, and despite the simmering resentment of a conquered people, the natives welcomed the influx of industry. Discussion about Alexander's tastes and particular requests were all the rage at social engagements in Dublin. My location outside the Pale was hardly convenient, yet every gentleman and lady of good breeding desired an invitation to view "Alexander's folly."

In the rusticated ground floor, beneath the ornate rooms of my piano nobile, in the heart of my structure, Alexander centred his laboratory.

Within, he forayed into secrets forbidden to all pious men.

***

She arrived after their wedding.

Tiny, delicate, and dressed in a silk dress edged in fur and studded with gems, Lady Claire Fitzhugh alit from the carriage as Alexander held her hand. She climbed my exterior steps and gazed at my columned portico with wide eyes and a pretty smile. I welcomed her with warm fires to guard against the slanting rain. The row of maids, footmen, butlers, and cooks curtseyed and bowed at her entrance. Her little speech coaxed smiles from them all, even the dour Francesco. Alexander drew her into the bedroom. I watched their coupling with interest, and recalled my birth of blood. So began weeks of dances and entertainments, which continued with evenings of cribbage, and harpsichord recitals by candlelight in the drawing rooms. Life filled me: from the mice tipping through fresh dust in the attic, to the gentlemen playing billiards in the conservatory, and the scullions dodging blows in the kitchen. For a time my inhabitants engaged my attention completely.

Eventually the bawdy company eased, and during the lulls Alexander retired to his hidden room, which was bound by charms and spells. Even I could not peer within, for it was fashioned to block prying spirits, and contain whatever he summoned.

During Alexander's absences, Claire rode an Arabian horse across the rough landscape. Francesco accompanied her on those jaunts, when not needed by Alexander, to guard her against local brutes. When inclement weather kept her indoors, which was often, she embroidered, or walked listlessly through the house, her hand upon her belly. On occasion she read books from Alexander's extensive library (except for the texts locked behind iron).

***

She screamed all night and I could do nothing.

Her bedroom reeked of fear and blood. The midwives discussed the birth in their native tongue, and despite my foreign design, I had roots deep within the land and their thoughts and speech were transparent to me.

They feared mother and child would die. I focused upon Claire's heartbeat, and willed it to beat. I sensed the small life's quest for delivery, but it weakened from the strain of the protracted labour.

Alexander withdrew to his sanctuary, and throughout the afternoon it was as if a thunderstorm brewed inside my walls. At once my foundations shuddered, the skulls under my heartstone shrieked, and even I overheard his urgent petition for assistance shoot into the ether.

A terrible darkness invaded me. I flinched from it, shocked and frightened by its touch. Deep inside I sensed claws, teeth, and an awful hungering need that wished only to corrupt and deceive. A pact was offered, accepted, and I could do nothing to prevent it.

When Alexander emerged from his laboratory, his black-stained fingers trembled, and he could speak to none.

Their son, Robert, surged out in a torrent of blood. Pale and weak, Claire could not nurse. Alexander arranged for a local wet-nurse, but she handed the child back after a couple of days and claimed her breasts had dried up. I heard whispers among the locals. Out of earshot of the priests who taught them in the hedgerows, they repeated primitive charms to their Saint-Goddess Bríd.

Claire paced the bedroom and rocked her screaming babe, while Alexander whipped his carriage to Dublin.

He returned with Helen Montgomery, chestnut-haired and wide-hipped. A recent widow, her family was respectable, humble, and Protestant. Her brown-eyed boy, James, crawled through my rooms and distracted Claire with his good-natured smiles. She loved him as a second son.

Sickly Robert Fitzhugh accepted Helen's milk, and Claire and Alexander were content for a while.

***

The changing weather and the bloom and decay of the gardens marked the seasons, as did regular tasks such as the beating of rugs, the polishing of the chandeliers, and the turning of mattresses.

Claire never carried another child to term, although three bloodied bundles were carried from her bedchamber. Despite the tears and heartbreak, Alexander did not enter another treaty with the forces he invoked to save Robert. The tiny sparks that failed to flourish within flesh floated free, and I caught them in the web of my magical structure. I welcomed two girls and a boy.

I grieved with Claire when she lay abed for weeks. I missed her laughter in the parlour and her light step upon my stairs. Alexander locked himself in his laboratory with increasing regularity, and the darkness he invited into me was a constant damp, dank spot that I tried to disregard.

Instead I focused upon the daily chores of the servants, the chatter of the children, and the ebb and flow of human life. Claire recovered, but her deprivations leeched her spirit of its previous vitality. Robert and James grew up like brothers: one red-haired and intense, the other dark and cheerful. Helen remained as companion and nurse to Claire. They confided in one another on all matters.

When Robert was ten years old, he stole the key to his father's hidden room. Fearful of a beating, James remained outside as lookout. I watched as Robert unlocked the door, unable to prevent his entrance to the shadowed realm. The door clanged behind him; James could not open it, and I could not see inside. After a long and anxious wait, Robert emerged, but I saw the mote that floated in his heart: the taint. James started at his friend's pallid features, but when Robert grinned, all seemed well.

In that moment, the unschooled Robert released a tendril of corruption from the room. It took root and began its slow and insidious assault upon me.

***

Everything changed after the argument.

Lightning speared from black clouds. The wind ripped tiles from the stables, and exposed the bucking horses to violent hail. Claire screamed accusations at Alexander. He responded with frosty disdain.

That evening Helen left, stiff-faced and red-eyed, with her luggage and a quiet James in tow. Robert waved goodbye from the bottom step, but refused to cry.

My family was riven. The corrosion ate into me as I mourned, helpless. Doors rattled in their frames; the servants cried out as shadows flitted after them down hallways, and all heard the wail of forsaken children.

Alexander retreated to his laboratory. Claire, maddened by solitude and the lonesome cry of her long-dead babes, took up a lamp and went down to her husband's detested sanctum--intent upon burning him from it if he refused her entry. There, the contamination was strongest, and my love for Claire twisted into resentment at her treason.

When Alexander ignored her hammering, she drew back the lamp, and for the first time I reached out and touched her mind. I showed her the evil feeding inside me, and her dead children's souls, which bloomed like lilies fed upon infected waters.

She froze, her eyes wide and devoid of reason.

Francesco stepped out of the shadows and removed the lamp from her lifeless arm. He guided her back to her bedchamber, and sat her upon the brocade coverlet. Quietly, he warned her against ever attempting such an action. He kissed her. She did not respond, or reject his advances.

The blight spread.

The storm passed, and I recovered, but I did not forget the memory of that night. The ability to touch the living lay within easy reach, and the voices that dwelled within me urged me to impose my will upon my residents. The power tempted me daily, and as the years passed I lapsed more often. Visitors complained of a sensation of cobwebs trailed upon bare skin as they traversed my corridors, or the sob of a child from a darkened closet whose door opened without assistance. Indistinct forms flickered behind reflections in mirrors. As dread secrets grew within me, they bled into the entire house until the atmosphere dulled.

Occasionally a cadre of men visited Alexander from Dublin and gathered in his laboratory. On those nights, my walls vibrated with summoned energies, and the rot quickened.

I watched over Claire, repentant for my cruelty, but she declined. She lost all appetite, and ignored her wardrobe and appearance. A doctor diagnosed a profound melancholia, and prescribed purgatives and cold baths. Alexander engaged a local woman to watch over her. Nora was kind to Claire, recognising the touch of a greater force upon the lady's mind. Yet, she pocketed the coin Francesco gave her to look the other way on the nights he slipped into Claire's chamber.

Most locals refused to stay a night under my roof, and guests visited less often. In a rare period of lucidity, Claire sent Robert away to England for schooling. Alexander reduced the staff. He embedded himself in his laboratory, and every day the taint strengthened while he conducted his experiments.

Eventually I grew accustomed to contact from the threshold of time and space, where shunned leviathans rested in a stupor and ignored the siphoning of dribs and drabs of their necrotising fluids. Soon I hungered for its taste. All who died under my roof were caught in my structural web, and they supped with me upon the stale nectar of insane gods and perverted angels.

Claire's father, a vicar, had a seizure upon seeing his dead granddaughter, still tangled in bloody swaddling, crawl from the empty fireplace in his bedroom and leave a trail of ashes. I latched upon the man's departing soul, and soon he hummed hymns to his grandchildren in tongues that had not been used in aeons.

I bound my family tight with love.

Alexander took note of the change in my demeanour. He attempted a ritual outside his laboratory to prove his theory that my framework now acted as an arcane container. During a lunar eclipse he summoned a door in my atrium, and stepped through into the Akashic library itself. He plundered its mystical records for knowledge barred to men for centuries.

Claire shambled through my empty hallways and whispered stories to her ghost children. She tossed slips of bloodied hair in her wake. Sometimes she confessed to me during her rambles as if I were her dearest comrade. Even Francesco avoided her company.

I loved her more than ever.

***

During the summer Robert returned, and with him came James, radiant and pure. Upon their arrival, Alexander informed them that Claire was holidaying with her sister in Malahide. In reality she was confined in a small room tight against my eves, with only Nora for company. From the secluded window, hallow-eyed and gaunt, Claire watched the young men climb the outer steps.

Robert and James had reunited at Cambridge. Their old friendship rekindled despite the drift of time and circumstances. The malign pressure that drove Robert to cruel pursuits and debauched pastimes eased while he consorted with James, and Robert exerted a fascination upon James like a charged lodestone.

My family was whole again.

One moonless night Alexander—his temples touched with grey—ordered all the staff from the house. A carriage filled with purposeful men arrived. They eschewed the laboratory; gateways into unnameable regions riddled my rooms.

Robed and hooded, Robert and James were led into the saloon and the circle of adepts. Braziers of charcoal and incense released soporific smoke. The chorus of souls in my walls sang chants in discordant melodies. Hellish shapes capered across the floor. Alexander initiated his son first. He drew the final symbol in blood upon Robert's forehead, and James backed away. Francesco seized the young man's arms, and refused him clemency.

My attention was focused on the ritual, so I did not notice when Nora's chin dipped to her chest, or remember the whiskey in her cup.

Claire, a gliding bald skeleton in a tattered grey dress, carried a lamp into the saloon. With her she brought silence. Robert froze, and Alexander grabbed his son to calm—or restrain—him. Francesco released James, and approached Claire with steady hands and a careful voice.

She tossed the oil lamp at Francesco. He erupted into flame, screamed, and then whirled around the room, seeking relief. He brushed heavy silk curtains and ran, arms outstretched to Alexander, who leaped back and knocked over a brazier.

Flames chased each other up Robert's robe. Alexander helped his son remove the burning cloth as the fire blackened my wallpaper and clawed up to the ceiling. The conflagration drove away the adepts, who scattered like dark leaves in a whirlwind. In the frenzy, James escaped.

Claire raised a knife, bright with reflected flames, above Alexander's back.

I could not permit it. I reached out, and punched her mind. She slumped to the floor.

Choking black smoke billowed from the fire. Alexander pushed his son from the room, and returned for Claire.

I felt both of them roast.

My windows exploded—a scream of pain—and the souls trapped inside me hammered for release.

Robert, scorched and weeping, stumbled down the steps into the garden as the inferno blazed through me. The laboratory collapsed with an exhalation of noxious spirits and a searing heat.

It purged me. My heartstone cracked, my magical net frayed, snapped, and faded. The souls that had abided with me for so many years swept upwards with the embers towards the bright heavens.

I burned for days.

No one attempted to rescue me. The locals spat on the ground in front of my charred steps and thanked their God for my destruction.

Only a shell remained, and I was much diminished.

The fire rid me of the corrupting madness. My pulse remained, a slow painful thud, under my chipped heartstone.

I slept.

I woke on occasion to notice the new height of the tree that grew in the stables, or to listen to the cattle call to one another as they grazed on the nettles that populated the old ballroom. A parliament of rooks took up residence in the remnants of the servants' quarters.

Occasionally local children dared each other to visit my ruins, and their bright presence recalled happier days. It was a painful pleasure to feel their curious hands touch my stained walls and scratch their names into my crumbling stone. Sometimes, I wished them to remain forever.

Other times I wished to strike them dead.

One day I woke from a dream of fire and blood to the sound of engines and shovels digging earth. The tree crowned the stables with a whispering green roof. Men in hard yellow helmets conversed by metal digging machines that issued black smoke.

I did not understand much, but I recognised the blue tracery of architectural drawings on large white scrolls.

I yearned for a fresh start free from memories.

Boots stamped the earth around me. Men and women in strange garb sat on tumbled walls, drank tea, ate sandwiches and watched a man with a polished trowel repair my heartstone.

The rooks circled down for scraps.

This time I would be good. I would protect all who lived within my walls. No taint would turn my actions against those I loved. An exclamation. Drops of blood fell upon soil-clogged sigils, and the man with the trowel started upright.

The bones beneath my heartstone shifted, and remembered their purpose. A slip of air breathed between animal teeth.

My pulse thumped faster.

I would be a home again for a new family, and we would be happy, forever.

This time I would ensure it.

∞∞∞

Maura McHugh, though born in the U.S., lives in Co. Galway, Ireland. She's a freelance web designer, consultant, and writer. She writes screenplays, short stories, poetry, and novels. Her writing has appeared in Flash me magazine, Cabinet des Fées, "Bone Mother", Fantasy anthology, Jabberwocky 3, Aoife's Kiss, and a script she co-wrote made it into the top twenty for the RTÉ Filmbase Short Script Awards. You can learn more about her and her projects at www.splinister.com

The Thing in the Woods
Nate Kenyon

As they approached the I-91 interchange, the argument took a nasty turn.

"I don't know what party you were at," Nyck said, "but the one I went to was supposed to be for the executives' club, not some swingers' group grope."

"That's not fair, and you know it. You asked me to talk to him."

"Talk, yes. Not slip your hand down the front of his pants."

"I did no such thing. Joe and I were discussing your career."

"So I suppose that look of rapture on his face was because of your shining conversational skills and not the way your tits looked in that blouse?"

Molly flashed him a withering look. "Sometimes you can be so crude. He's an old man, Nyck."

"Not old enough. I bet he could still get it up pretty good."

"Will you please stop?"

"And then, when it was time to leave and you said you wanted to stay a while longer, Christ, it was like a neon sign blinking over your head saying, for a good time call—"

"Will you please--I wish you would just please SHUT UP!"

The slightly hysterical edge in her voice brought an abrupt end to the tirade. Nyck sat stiffly upright next to her, his white-knuckled hands gripping the wheel of the Volvo. His shoulders strained at the seams of his tuxedo jacket. Then he sighed, flexed his hands and let his shoulders slump. "Fuck," he said. He glanced

quickly at her, then back at the road. "What a night."

Molly knuckled at the ache behind her eyes and stared out into the darkness. It was past midnight, and they were the only car on the highway. The headlights cut a narrow path through the black, white lane dashes flicking rhythmically past, one after another. It had begun to drizzle. Wipers scraped across the glass, smearing the shadows of the trees on either side of the road.

She glanced at the glove compartment and imagined the gun cradled inside, patiently waiting, barrel's eye peering out at the darkness.

No. Don't think about that. Not now.

She let her head fall back against the seat. The motion of the car rocked her gently, and she felt herself drifting off. No matter how Nyck treated her, she was unable to sustain the hot flare that burned in her stomach. Until recently, she had still held out hope that he would find the strength to change. It seemed impossible that the years had changed him so completely.

They'd met at a Florida State seminar on English literature. She'd needed it for her major; he was simply looking for a credit to get him past the finish line. He was athletic, charming, good-looking. All the girls loved him. She was small and shy and bookish. She never understood what he'd seen in her.

But they'd fallen hard for each other very quickly. She'd never been one to force anything, but with Nyck, that was fine. He seemed to pull something inside her out into the light, and she liked the feeling.

The expression that passed across her mother's face the first time she'd met Nyck was priceless. Like she'd tasted something that had spoiled. Molly had never done anything to make her mother disapprove of her, not in all her years growing up. And that, in the end, had only made her more resolute in her decision. The relationship suddenly turned into a rebellion. She took every opportunity to throw him in her mother's face, saying, yes, this is me. This is what I want.

After graduation they rented an apartment above a bakery in St. Petersburg, and the sweet smell of freshly-cooked challah bread filled their bedroom each morning. Looking back, she thought those days had the fuzzy, dizzying quality of a dream. Nyck had focused his attentions on her in a way that was both flattering and slightly overwhelming. He did everything with her, for her: helped pick her clothes, her friends, her music and movies and restaurants. Because of him, she became ever trendier, more sophisticated, more worldly. Nobody had ever wanted her this way, and she struggled to understand how to deal with it.

She spent her days shelving books in a library down the street, while he worked for a man who sold insurance out of a little shop in Clearwater. At night they would eat Chinese food while sitting cross-legged on the floor beside the packing box that served as a coffee table, and talk about buying land and raising a family.

A year later he proposed to her on a camping trip to Mt. Katahdin in Maine. Instead of being silver-screen romantic, it was awkward and sweet. He dropped the ring and she was unable to stop giggling, even as he slid it on her finger. They made love on a bed of pine needles and she got all scratched up and itchy, but she didn't much care. All she wanted was to feel him inside her.

When he came he grabbed her hair and his mouth opened but no sound came out; every muscle and tendon turned to rock. The scream she kept waiting for had been bitten back too hard, and when she kissed him, she tasted blood.

A short while after that, they were married in a small ceremony in his hometown in New Hampshire, with their parents and her brother as best man. Her mother seemed to have come around at last. They returned to Florida, but she could tell Nyck's heart wasn't in it, and soon he began talking about moving back home again. It was what he wanted, she told herself. He was her husband, and she must obey his wishes.

She could not recall the precise moment when the smell of challah bread in the morning began to sicken her. But Nyck kept buying it, and she kept making French toast for their breakfast, too afraid to tell him.

They moved away from the little bakery and into a larger apartment in Portland. The smell eventually left her clothes, but their lives grew more and more cluttered as Nyck began his rise up the ladder in a larger firm. Though she wanted to look for a new job, he insisted she quit working. He was bringing in nearly six figures now, and they could afford to buy a house and start talking about children. He wanted lots of them. She would not tell him no. They tried to get pregnant every night, whether she was interested or not.

As the days passed and she didn't conceive, she saw less and less of him. He would stay later and later at the office, and there were times when she wondered seriously if he was having an affair. But she began to realize that his career was not going exactly the way he wanted, and when he was passed over for another promotion, she saw the change in him more clearly. The late hours he kept began to feel more desperate.

When she told him she was finally pregnant, he smiled like a man who had found out he was the butt of a joke. She didn't find out until days later that he had lost his job, and had been spending his time on the road, looking for work.

***

Molly hardly realized she had drifted off until she was jarred awake again. Her head thudded dully, and her eyes felt filled with sand.

The car shuddered over uneven road. She looked at her husband. He sat hunched over the wheel, peering out into the darkness. The green lights of the dash lit his face from below, stretching the shadows around his jowls and eyes.

She turned to stare out the windshield. The rain had picked up, and the wipers worked harder to flick away a sheet of water with each pass. She shook away the memories. Probably the weather and her aching head, and of course the argument. All had combined to make her feel quite nostalgic indeed.

The party that night had been held at a sprawling country estate overlooking the Kennebec River, about forty-five minutes from their house, which was located in the suburbs outside of Portland. It was a fairly quick shot up the pike and across a couple of short city roads. Forty-five minutes, maybe an hour in this weather. They should be on the last leg of the turnpike now.

But what she saw through the rain was some back road lined with brush, hardly wide enough for two cars to pass each other. A light mist blew in ghostly white tendrils across the asphalt, merging with the skeletal branches of the trees to form a seething, shifting illusion of solid ground. The headlights were practically useless.

Thump. Her teeth came together with a click. The car rocked on its springs. Another pothole, then a series of them; thump-thud-thud. What an awful place, she thought. "Where are we?"

Nyck was sweating lightly. "I decided to take another way home."

"This is like somebody's driveway."

"So now you decide to put your two cents in?"

"I fell asleep—"

"No shit."

"Okay," she said carefully, "so you got off the turnpike."

He glanced over at her. What did he see when he looked at her now? She wasn't sure she wanted to know.

The road obviously hadn't seen much attention for quite some time. The car shuddered, running over cracks and holes and ragged gaps in the pavement. She hadn't seen a house, a mailbox, or another road. She hadn't even seen another car since she woke up. It was as if they had dropped off the face of the earth.

There were roads like this, she knew. Places where you could get lost and never see anyone for hours, huge stretches of nothing but pine and oak and a few squirrels and bears. But this close to Portland? It was hard to believe. Unless Nyck had gotten them turned around somehow. Unless they were moving away from the city, or any other civilized place.

The mist seemed to dissolve whole sections of ground just ahead of them as the rain drummed steadily, and the wipers worked harder to keep up. "I think we should turn around," she said. "Maybe we can retrace our steps."

"I know what I'm doing." This time he did not look at her at all. She could see his hands tightening on the wheel, his protruding knuckles like bones in the dashboard lights.

"Look, I'm sorry about tonight, okay?"

"Forget it."

"I think we should talk—"

"Jesus." The word was expelled from his mouth like something bitter. "You can't leave anything alone, can you? Know what I think? I think you can't stand being with me anymore. Maybe you wish we never got married in the first place."

The silence hung between them like a third passenger.

"Maybe my life didn't turn out exactly as I pictured it," Molly said. "I know yours didn't either. The question is, what do we do now?"

He glanced at her in surprise. They were coming up on a turn. He was driving much too fast as something big and dark lumbered out of the shadows and directly in front of the car.

She screamed as he twisted the wheel and they slid sideways across wet pavement. The shape loomed up before the sweeping headlights, huge and black and dripping. She saw fur and the flash of something white, and the bright yellow glint of its eyes.

A jarring thud threw her up against the dashboard and the car swung violently around, rear end swapping places with the front. Tires shrieked; the car slid off the shoulder and came to a sudden stop facing back the way they had come, engine stalled and facing an empty road.

The headlights were dimmer than before. One of the bulbs must have shattered. The mist swirled.

"My God," Nyck whispered after a moment. He was sitting in the same position, gripping the steering wheel with both hands. "I hit it head-on, didn't I? I fucking hit it." He slammed his palms into the wheel. "Shit!"

"What was it?"

"A bear, I think. Isn't that what it looked like to you?"

"I don't know," Molly said. It hadn't looked much like a bear at all, in fact. It had looked like nothing she had ever seen before. She took a deep, shuddering breath. Her breasts ached where she had slammed into the seatbelt, and she caressed her slightly rounded belly. She shivered, weak from the sudden rush of adrenaline, her stomach clenching and unclenching like a tight, wet fist in her guts.

The engine ticked softly, the sound mixing with the rain pattering on the hood.

Outside the car, nothing moved.

Nyck kicked the emergency brake and opened the door, letting in a swirl of cold, damp air.

"Wait a minute," she said. "What if it's not dead?"

"I was going fifty miles an hour. I want to check on the car." He slammed the door, pulled the jacket of his tuxedo up around his head and ran to the front of the Volvo, crouching in the mud.

She cracked her window, eyes scanning slowly up the road, expecting to see the rounded hump of the bear carcass. But she saw nothing except thick underbrush and shadows and that seething blanket of mist.

That was no bear. It had been too big for a dog, and it hadn't been the right shape for a deer or moose. It had been huge. And something else--she couldn't be sure, because everything happened so fast--but she could have sworn it had been standing upright.

Nyck was muttering to himself. She called out the half-open window. "Is it serious?"

"I think we're leaking fluid. The grill's pretty messed up, but I don't see ..." his voice was muffled through the rain. "Wait, a little blood on the fender, some hair ... Jesus, it smells bad. Like rotten meat or something."

She could smell it now through the open window, a stench like old garbage or a dead animal lying in the sun. She almost got out of the car, but something held her back. If she got out, she had the strangest feeling she would never get back in.

Nyck wrenched open the hood. She couldn't see anything through the windshield now except chipped paint, but she could hear him poking around inside the engine.

That smell...

"Wait," Nyck was saying. "I heard something." He closed the hood and stepped away from the car, and she called out one more time. He peered in at her through the half-open window. His jacket hooded his dripping face so she couldn't make out his expression. "What's the problem?"

Suddenly she didn't want to admit she was frightened. Not to him, not to a man who saw only a hysterical woman who couldn't get along on her own.

"Nothing," she said. "I just thought you might be cold."

He peered at her for another moment, then turned and began to walk purposefully up the road. She watched until the mist and the darkness swallowed him up. Then she opened the glove compartment and fumbled around inside.

She wasn't sure of the exact day he had bought the gun. Maybe it had been before they had moved to their house, but she only learned about it months later. He showed it to her after they had watched a news magazine special about carjackers, and he tried to pass it off as protection for both of them. But she knew it meant something else. For her, it was a threat. For him, she thought, it was a talisman against a darkness deeper than he was willing to face.

When she finally found it tucked among the maps and travel pamphlets, she discovered that her hands were shaking too badly to pick it up. She clutched its oily smoothness, its unfamiliar weight, and dropped it on the floor at her feet.

What am I thinking of doing, exactly?

She stared at the spot where Nyck had disappeared. Tears of frustration welled up and she angrily fisted them away, blinking hard until they stayed down. She wanted to go home. But they couldn't go home and forget all about tonight, could they? It was far too late for that.

Something slipped out of the bushes to her right.

One moment there was nothing but mist and rain and then there was something, not a clear recognizable shape but something dark and upright, moving with a speed and agility that seemed impossible for its size, loping across the open, lit space in front of the car.

One second it was there, the next it was gone. All she saw were rustling bushes on the opposite side of the road in the dim light, and then even those slowed and became still.

Her throat suddenly dry, she swallowed with an audible click. What had she seen in that split second as it passed her by? A face, turning to peer in at her through the glass?

Pulse hammering, she scooted over the gearshift and into the driver's seat, pumping the gas pedal and turning the key. The engine ground, turning over once, twice, not catching. Frantically she pumped the pedal again and listened to the engine turn over. She smelled gas.

Molly looked out the driver's side window at the place where the thing had disappeared. Imagined it peering at her between the leaves. Rain pounded the pavement and drummed on the roof.

Nyck materialized out of the downpour a moment later, shouting and gesturing at her as he approached down the center of the road. She scooted back over to her side of the car.

"What the hell were you doing?" he said after he'd gotten back into the car. He rubbed his dripping face with the soaked tuxedo jacket and then tossed the jacket into the backseat. His hair was plastered down around his forehead. "Were you going to leave me here? Is that it?"

"Why would I do that?"

"Don't get cute with me, goddamnit. I know what you're thinking. I used to be a big shot, right? And now I'm kissing up to Kiernan, a fucking sales executive, for Christ's sake, just to get hired back at my old firm."

"It's a job, Nyck. A junior rep is better than nothing. You were looking for a long time."

"I know it's a job. But I might as well be washing toilets. And you know it, don't you? You fucking know it."

"Calm down—"

"I bet you did want to fuck him, didn't you? Is that what tonight was all about? Maybe that baby isn't even mine. Am I right? I'd fucking kill you before I let that happen. You hear me?"

He'd swung around to face her and raised his fist. His face was purple and the veins stuck out on his neck. The words she was going to say, something recycled and familiar, caught in her throat. "Get out," she said instead.

She was staring at his hands. Those black, wiry hairs on them. He had the same black hairs sprouting across his upper arms. If she closed her eyes she could see them as he held himself rigid over her in bed, the way he did when he fucked her. Lately he liked to put it in her ass, and when she said no it seemed to excite him even more.

Violence clung to the air like a scent. Nyck was still frozen with a fist in the air, a very odd expression on his face. Almost like shock. *Why hasn't he swung at me?* She wondered. *He wants to, I know he does.*

His eyes weren't on her face, but somewhere below. She was surprised to feel the pebbled grip of the gun in her hand, the oiliness of the trigger under her finger. She couldn't remember reaching down to pick it up.

She was pointing it right at him.

She could smell the metal and she felt her blood thrum in her veins.

"Molly—"

"Get out," she said again. Her hands were steady now. She cocked the hammer back.

For a moment she thought he would refuse, but then he opened the door and slipped backward out into the mist.

She opened her own door and stood up, feeling the cool air caress her face. The rain had eased once again and the smell of mud and the leaves of the trees widened her nostrils.

At the shoulder of the road, behind where Nyck stood staring at her in shock, the bushes rustled.

"I'm going to fucking kill you," Nyck growled, his confidence trickling back. He took a half-step toward her. "How dare you point that thing at me? Fucking bitch."

Molly came around the front end of the car. She braced the butt-end of the gun with her other palm. She did not look down at her belly, did not take her eyes from Nyck's face. But she felt it there, waiting for her to do something.

The creature stepped out of the woods. It was at least seven feet tall and covered in black, wiry fur. It stood upright like a man, but had the face of a great ape; the thing's hands were huge and flat as dinner plates, covered in hair except for the palms, which were deeply creased. Dirt ringed its fingernails, as if it had been digging in the mud. Its legs were thickly muscled, toenails curled down and gripping the muddy grass like bear claws.

It bared its inch-long, yellow fangs at her.

She closed her eyes and pulled the trigger.

The gun cracked and bucked in her hands, and she smelled oil and smoke. When she opened her eyes Nyck had stumbled and she pulled the trigger again and again, the sound of the gun mingling with a low howl that came from the thing from the woods as it raised its hairy arms, threw back its head and screamed into the mist.

Finally the hammer fell with a click on an empty chamber.

Molly blinked. Rain once again shook the hanging branches of the trees. The mist swirled and eddied and flowed across the open spaces, turning the road into a long, narrow tunnel that led off the face of the earth.

Nyck lay face down in a pool of blood. The fingers of his right hand twitched. He sighed, as if something heavy had been lifted from him, and then the creature had him by the shoulders. It picked him up as lightly as a pillow and tucked him under one arm, then turned its yellow eyes on her and bared its fangs again. Blood dripped on the asphalt. Drip, drip, drip.

Her hand was numb. Her face was numb. The smell of the thing was like a thousand bloody, rancid corpses in a killing field. She dropped the gun and covered her mouth with her hand, and stepped back as the creature slipped noiselessly through the bushes and disappeared.

Molly waited for another few moments but heard nothing more. The smell began to fade. She turned to the car, slipped trembling into the driver's seat and locked the doors. Then she dug her phone out of her purse with shaking hands and hit a number on the speed dial.

Joe Kiernan came on the line, sounding groggy. He barely got out a word before she started talking.

"I shot him," she said in a rush. "He knew the baby wasn't his. He watched us together all night. I had to do it or he was going to kill me."

She listened to Joe's voice. He spoke for a few minutes and she listened carefully. Joe wanted her to make a note of where it had happened and drive away. He told her he would send someone to take care of everything.

Then he asked her if she was all right.

She hesitated, glancing back out the rain-streaked window to the edge of the road. The smell was gone now, and the bushes were still.

"Yes," she said. "I'm…just a little rattled, that's all."

After they hung up Molly got out of the car. She kicked the gun into the grass, out of sight. Then she walked over and knelt, reached down and caressed the huge, misshapen footprint she found there, pictured those claws in her mind as the cold mud squelched between her fingers. She remembered the screams and the blood.

Then she locked it all up and put it away for good.

Molly turned her back on the woods and returned to the car. A quick twist of the key and the engine roared to life. She gave it a little gas, eased out the clutch and pulled into the road, driving slowly, carefully, back the way she had come.

She was a long way from home.

◊◊◊◊◊

Nate Kenyon grew up in a small town in Maine with dark nights and long winters to feed his interest in writing. He earned a BA in English from Trinity College in Hartford, CT in 1993, winning awards in playwriting and fiction.

His dark fiction stories have appeared in various magazines and in the horror anthology Terminal Frights. Kenyon has worked at the Brookline Public Library in Brookline, Mass. and the Boston College Law School as their Director of Marketing & Communications. He is a member of the Horror Writers Association and International Thriller Writers.

Learn more at www.natekenyon.

AN EX-CON on the run from his own shattered past…

A WOMAN taken against her will…

A YOUNG MAN consumed by rage…

AND A TOWN on the edge of darkness.

In White Falls, a horrifying truth is about to be uncovered that will unleash an ancient evil. Some secrets should remain buried…

natekenyon.com

BE THE DARKNESS
TOM PICCIRILLI
KEN BRUEN

You think running a night club is easy.

Fucking re-think, pal.

Back then, you needed two things to run a great place.

And I'm talking great….As in fucking amazing, the kind of joint that the punters cream their pants to get into.

First you needed cajones… balls as big as Sinatra's voice… and we had him. I'm not shitting you… ole Frankie and I, we went way back. His mom, as dangerous and feral a bitch as you'd ever meet, she used to pat my head, go,

"You watch out for my Frankie, hear?"

I heard, it was hard not to… she'd a voice like a damn foghorn… and Frank, god rest his wicked soul, wasn't afraid of nothing…'cept maybe Ava and his mom.

When he married that skin and bones job, the Farrow cunt, I was one of the very few to be able to go,

"The fuck you playing at?"

The second essential was… heat… yeah, being heeled, carrying a piece all the time.

You go to the restroom, you bring the piece, you get a broad into the sack, bring the piece.

One thing I learnt in here, you keep your head and your voice real low.

It's why you won't find me in the history books, or the hundreds of books on Frank. He used to kid me,

"What's with the invisible routine?"

Frank, with his massive ego, his thirst for recognition, could never understand anyone who would shun the spotlight.

But I knew that to be visible was to be vulnerable.

Right, Joe?

Ah man, even now, all those years on, I nearly smile at that.

Joe.

Ah Jesus, the memories come rolling back and me eyes, dammit all to hell, they're wet as the Emerald Isle I never got to visit.

I came from a family of Micks, all shamrocks and Irish whiskey, rosary beads and superstitions, steeped in a lore that was as guilt-ridden as it was exhilarating. The streets of Brooklyn, we didn't play cowboys and Indians… no, it was the Irish freedom fighters against The Brits.

At least, on the streets of Flatbush and Bay Ridge, for once, The Brits got nailed and good.

My career choices were limited… cop, legbreaker, or bootlegger. As my old man was doing a stretch for armed robbery, the blues weren't ever going to be an option.

And, you grow up shite poor, you're going to want the green, no pun intended, and fast, and mountains of it.

Booze, 'tis in our heritage, and if you can make money out of it as well as all the other kicks, is there a choice?

Not for me, not ever.

I started early, runner for the local Mick mafia, and worked me way up to managing one of the hottest joints in New York City when I was only twenty-eight. Sure, I did lots of rough shite, a lot of heads got busted, but you didn't get to run a top club by being Mr. Nice Guy.

I didn't do nice.

Don't do a whole lot of it now, either.

The name of the place, we called it Club Darkness, and we got everybody, and I mean it, everybody... all the nobs, the mayor, Broadway producers, New York tycoons, the Hollywood elite, the newspaper guys, everybody. We had that magic ingredient, damn straight... word of mouth.

We even had a motto, and I figure it had a lot to do with our rep. Be the darkness.

Corny as fook, huh?

Shite worked though.

It promised all sorts of forbidden pleasures, alluring sins, stuff you could only fantasize about. And buddy, lemme tell you... we delivered... fucking A.

You wanted a black or a yellow or a red broad, we got her, and no one paid no never mind. You wanted some hard junk, some uppers, downers, beauties, powder... no problem, and we were discreet.

Anyone shooting his mouth off about the club's activities, we had a goon squad, serious damage limitation guys. They took the mouth into the back alley and guess what... he stopped mouthing, maybe for a while, maybe forever.

It was magic... dark magic.

Didn't come cheap.

Does it ever?

And we had Frank.

Yeah, word was out, Frank liked to drop by.

But the vicious black magic, the serious mojo, it didn't come from Joe, but it started with him. He

brought it with him one Saturday night, wrapped in mink and wearing pearls, with blue glimmering eyes and a laugh that made men turn away from their action, their money, their bottles and needles.

Everyone, even those already busy in the private back rooms, came out to take a peek at her.

My mother, she called a woman like that "hellfire on high heels"... my father, he'd once told me, "A lass like that, son, you never light her cig, you never get that close."

But who listens to an old fook stuck up in the pen?

Not me... not usually... but that night, I thought the old man might finally be right about something.

Joe, in his finest black suit, wearing a bow-tie, Jay-sus, introduced her around to the boys... her name, I heard him say, was Mara.

They turned it over on their tongues, couldn't get enough of just the sound of it... Mara, Mara, all of them vying for attention. Hoping she was a working girl, and they could cop the number from me or Joe.

I worked it with my own lips. Mara. Joe stood back and watched as they bought champagne for her, danced, and yes, lit her cigs.

I kept back in the wings, filling out paperwork, ordering the liquor, checking the cash flow, seeing the back rooms were full and the dope was all right, the girls doing their jobs. Making sure that whenever I was in Joe's sights, I quickly moved on.

I didn't want to meet her... that laugh, even from across the club, it called to something dark and malignant inside of me. The very worst part.

All night long, as I watched from the alcoves, from behind the bar, and propped in the doorway of my office, the thing inside me stirred and made the blood rush in my ears. I started throwing back the whiskey. I knew how to hold it, and I knew when I was pushing. I pushed and threw it down.

Joe kept sighting me up, starting over like he wanted to talk, wanted me to actually come round and visit with her.

Shite that.

Joe was short for Giovanni, a Sicilian who ran a small book outfit in Hell's Kitchen, always calling on one saint or another. Some I knew, some I didn't. Sicilians, the only people even more superstitious than us Micks... must've been from living in the shadow of so many active volcanoes.

I thought, Joe, you're a jealous fook, even worse than me, so why are you parading her out before the swine?

Unless he wanted to be rid of her.

Circled by gents, she glanced up once and found my eyes. A voice at the back of my head told me to go grab my .38, my backup .32, arm up for war. Another voice said, You're caught, you stupid Mick, you're invisible no longer. She's seen you now.

You can fight your fate and let it drag you screaming along, or you can man up, fire up, step up, and meet it head on. Had to admit, I wondered what Frank might do. Or his mother.

So I walked to Mara, through the ring of admirers, the boys who knew better than to say a word to me about moving in on their territory. One tried to edge me out with his shoulder and I elbowed the punter in the kidneys. When he stopped gagging, he and the rest lit out. Joe was nowhere near.

Her perfume was a mixture of old money, unfiltered Camels, fat doobies, and heady sex. She stood two inches over me... hellfire in high heels... and I wanted to hook her in my arms and drag her to my corner of the club. She saw the burn in me and it widened her smile, made her say,

"You'd be the man that runs the show."

My retort, not as suave as I would have liked,

"This show, anyway."

Truth, if nothing more.

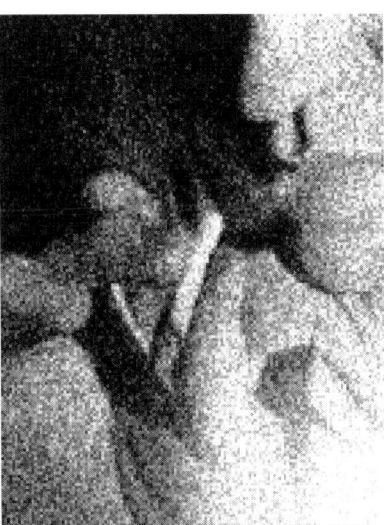

We danced and drank, and Joe never did show himself again. All that time trying to hound me out into the open, and now that I was, he'd taken to hiding. We had to have a talk about that. I wondered why he'd brought her to the club tonight. Wasn't until later that I started to question if she'd been the one who'd brought him.

She noticed how the shoulder holster kept throwing off the way I moved, gave a laugh that was both lovely and set my teeth on edge, said,

"You dance like a man carrying hardware."

Again, lacking sophistication and polish,

"Because I am."

"You ice anyone lately?"

I had and said, "Not today."

Leave the priss talk to Frank and the rest who could make it work for them.

There'd been women before. Women I'd wanted and had to have. Sometimes they were married women of social standing, of blueblood heritage, and I had to send the boys around to clop a husband's ears. Most of the men loosened their hold by then. One punter didn't and wound up going into the East River. They found him washed up on a Jersey City shore a week later. I took what I wanted.

There'd been women.

But none who'd managed to squeeze my heart in her hands so quickly and easily, so deftly, as if it was the thing she was born to do... and to do specifically to me.

A few minutes later, in my arms, she was kissing my throat, humming against my flesh, telling me things about myself I didn't know or had long since forgotten... at first, bits of memory that had been tucked away, which she drew out with a giggle. And me thinking, Did I tell her or did she tell me?

Her voice a croon in my ear, and me spilling words back to her, but distantly, as if I was far away from my own voice. Soon my head twirled with my past, a skull jammed full of bad moments and blood, my sins laid out before me… thought, There's no way she can know this about me, I must be losing it, all this jigging, with my nuts on fire… what have I been saying?

Even a man like me can talk too much, and it had happened before. Try as you might, you can't always be on guard. You let slip. You make mistakes. I figured I must be making them now, and I looked in those blue eyes again, and was startled to note they were blue no longer, but black and gleaming. Reminded me of my own.

The weight of the city bore down, the charge in the club making my fillings ache. I started growing sweaty and light-headed, took it for lust and need, thought the whiskey was catching up, all the thrashing blood in my veins. Dancing the way we were, it was the way to fill a young man's night, and I'd started to leave my green days behind. She seemed to wear away at the veneer I'd spent so long building, to get to the raw meat and marrow beneath.

She stroked my cheek, stepped back and put a few feet between us, said,

"You taste sweet, you fill me with hate."

Took that to mean she didn't like me, and my heart actually sank, the way it would for any punter. Daft, I must be going daft. The effect she had on me proved again why it's best to stay out of the light, where your vulnerability shows up in the glare.

But she went back to nuzzling, pressed her cheek to my chest, and sighed, then said,

"He was right about you."
"Who? Joe?"
"Yes, he told me you had no heart, and you don't."
"It's there. It just doesn't beat often."

My attempt at humor. I never could get them laughing much.

"What beats isn't your heart.

It's a lump of your petty whims and jealousies, your thefts and your bitter aches."

Tried to discourage that line of talk and said, "More whiskey? Another cigarette?"

That laugh, like a knife in the ribs, making me wince and making me hard. She told me,

"More embracing. I like the touch of you. The rot inside you. More than most men."

Didn't know what the fuck that meant and said,

"The fuck does that mean?"
"It means I fancy your wickedness."

A lot of women had said that, one way or another, but none with as much elation.

"And you truly like that?"
"No, I hate it, because I need it. We all hate it, but we have no choice but to lie in the arms of bastards such as you. I need you."
"Are you stone mad, Mara?"
Fuckin' wild chick.

And then I must've gone a touch mad myself because I saw the thing inside of her reach out to what was inside of me.

At first I thought maybe she'd been shot, and that her blood had come streaking forth toward me. I even put my hand up across my eyes so as not to get blood in them.

Then watched that red thread still moving from the center of her chest and whipping in a straight line towards me. When it touched, the blackness inside me crooned and my mouth started to water. Said,

"The fuck?"

She took my hand and led me out into the night and down the city streets to a high class building, up six flights to an apartment…. It was dark and empty and cold in there, and I didn't recognize it as we made love, until the red thread between us and began to glow and I saw I was in my own home.

Said again,
"The fuck?"

But we get along in the world. We've a great capacity for accepting vast amounts of pain and perplexity and disorientation. Maybe we even seek it out. It's not easy to drive a man insane because he's always lived on the edge anyway. That last inch over is the longest there is. We struggle on, and mad sex and whiskey helps, so long as we're sated in the end.

She salved me and worked me and laid hard up against me... she whispered and hissed and eased my disbelief and stole my sins.

No, didn't steal them... snared them, shared them, rifled through them, licked them one by one.

It was a heady night, a high I'd never reached before with pills or powder or the needle or anything else I'd ever tried. My heart hammering for hours, the bed covered in sweat, leaving me shaken, my legs too weak to keep me standing, and my teeth chattering.

In the morning, Mara was gone, but she'd left a note:

"We live in a complex, brutal world, and only women of celestial beauty and men of provocative cruelty make us strong."

Cryptic, that. Had a crazed moment where I thought, What would Frank's mom make of all this?

First thing, went out to find Joe to ask him about the dark magic, the serious mojo. Went 'round to his place on Fifty-Seventh, the book office, his favorite luncheon, but couldn't find him. He was playing invisible now. Kept hunting him, asking the boys, his employees, the women he'd known before Mara. Took a wild chance and found him in a back pew at St. Pat's.

Sat beside him, heard him actually whispering his prayers, holding a rosary. Asked him, point blank,

"What have you done?"

Looked up from his prayers long enough to eye me and said,

"I had to."

"Because I'm a man of provocative cruelty?"

"You are."

"And have no heart?"

"No, you don't."

Saying it not in judgment but as simple fact. Couldn't fault him for that, laying it on the line. Joe knew me and I knew him. We came from a world where you couldn't trust anyone, not even your best friends, and there was no use getting angry with some punter who'd fooked you over and brought misery into your life.

"Where's she from?"

"I don't know."

"What happens now?"

"It's going to get worse."

"How?"

He couldn't say and I was glad. Didn't really want to know, not after looking deep in his face. Realizing that Joe wasn't the same man I'd known for all these years... everything I liked about him was gone.

His hard edge, his charm, his willingness to throw down into a fight for almost no reason. His guts, his cajones, his heat....

He stared at me from the far side of oblivion and I thought, There, that's where I'm headed for.

Mara walked in, moved to Joe, and didn't even give me a glance of recognition.

"Mara," I said, my voice almost breaking into a whine, fook that, because whatever had happened last night, I wanted more.

The way she'd shared and snared my evils, drained them of their color. Worked them in her, while the red thread connected us. Like getting high on the needle, even when you had no veins left to shoot it into.

Mara turned then and our eyes met, and I knew then it wasn't her, not the Mara I'd been with last night, not mine. This was Joe's Mara.

I said,

"Who the fook are you?"

She responded with a grin that chilled me and made the skin between my shoulders crawl. Told me,

"I have many sisters."

Jay-sus.

That night, Joe, sipping the best whiskey in the house, smiled a thousand-watt smile, but there was no charm there, all it was was his teeth, and his eyes were black and near-dead. He was alone. Mara, neither mine nor his, was in the club. In the barest whisper, he said,

"I'm in love. And I can't stop myself. I'm vanishing, memory by memory, and I'm afraid."

I was wearing both guns and had a pigsticker switchblade in my back pocket, and still I felt defenseless, and nearly as chewed up and spat out as him.

He wandered away from me, wandered the club in a daze for a time. Heard his gun go off and found him sitting in my office chair, his brains poured out across my desk. Cleaned him up double-jig quick time. Had the music play louder, the girls score the old men to keep them busy, gave a few rounds of drinks away for free. The crowd barely noticed the slight ripple of trouble, and the next night, no one cared at all.

Mara, my Mara, found me again and again, even when I tried to hide. There was no point in staying in my apartment, door locked. No reason to sit in the gloom of my office staring at the desk top, wondering if I should just do it.

She found me whenever she wanted, and brought me out to dance, and then supped on my sins and stole my darkest moments one and all. Soon, I put my guns up. Didn't have the heart for them... the wickedness, the cajones to pull the trigger any more.

Frank stopped coming around too. The last time I saw him, he said, "What the hell's happened to you, you Mick bastard? Where'd your balls go?"

Trying to get a rise out of me. Felt a slight stir inside, looking at him right then, the bloated prick, but it swept off almost immediately.

Just smiled, let that be my answer.

Could feel myself drifting already, becoming less of what I was. Not invisible, but hollow. Endlessly empty, the world growing dimmer and beyond my reach. Full of nothing within or without, except eternal distance and black space.

Be the darkness...

Think on that to the yawning grave.

⋄⋄⋄⋄⋄

Ken Bruen is the acclaimed and popular author of such powerful crime novels as AMERICAN SKIN, LONDON BOULEVARD (soon to be a major motion picture), the Brant series, and the Jack Taylor series, including THE GUARDS, THE DRAMATIST, and the Edgar Award-nominated PRIEST. Learn more at www.kenbruen.com.

Tom Piccirilli is the author of twenty novels including THE COLD SPOT, THE MIDNIGHT ROAD, and THE DEAD LETTERS. He's a four-time winner of the Bram Stoker Award and has been a finalist for the World Fantasy Award, the International Thriller Writers Award, and Le Grand Prix de L'Imagination. Learn more at www.tompiccirilli.com.

The Haunted Wood

Tools and Toys

for the MAGICALLY MINDED

Handmade altars, wands, staves, staffs, athames, chalices, besoms, runes, ogham, boxes and more.

Rare and Unique Woods including:

Almond wood, Holly, English Yew, and Irish Bog Oak, and much more.

New England's preminent Pagan/Wiccan resource.

visit us today at:

www.hauntedwoodcrafts.com

...

graphix studio
logo design • screen printed clothing
design & sales   drew davis
603•969•4987   anamgraphix@aol.com

NOX ARCANA

MUSIC FROM THE SHADOWS

Haunting, gothic soundscapes, ghostly choirs and pulse-pounding orchestrations inspired by classic horror literature from H.P. Lovecraft, Bram Stoker and Edgar Allan Poe. Each cd contains 21 tracks.

For music samples and other cds, visit:
WWW.NoxArcana.com

WWW.BRIANKEENE.COM

$7.99 Each
New Horror!

**SHROUD PUBLISHING
IS A
PROUD MEMBER
OF THE HORROR WRITERS' ASSOCIATION
AND THE NEW ENGLAND HORROR WRITERS**

PLEASE SUPPORT OUR AUTHORS AND ARTISTS

WWW.SHROUDMAGAZINE.COM

THANK YOU!

GRIMOIRES AND TOMES

Book Reviews

DUMA KEY, Stephen King
Review by I.E. Lester

Edgar Freemantle was a successful businessman; he had it all. He'd spent twenty years building his construction company into a multi-million dollar concern. He could look at the twin cities of Minneapolis-St. Paul and see a horizon that he was, to a significant degree, responsible for.

All of this matters little when an accident resulted in serious brain damage—and his losing his right arm. Following his release from the hospital, and the breakup of his marriage, he decides to leave the cold climate of Minnesota for the Florida Keys - a quiet place to allow his mind and body to heal.

Upon the advice of his doctor, Freemantle takes up painting - a hobby he had not indulged in since college days. He quickly discovers he has a gift for it. Following some persuasion on the part of his daughter, Ilse, and new friend Wireman, a former lawyer who managed to survive putting a bullet into his own head, Freemantle agrees to show his paintings to a local art gallery. Their faith in his work is justified; the gallery instantly offers him an exhibition.

But being a Stephen King story, this gift is for more than just creating beautiful works of art. Freemantle slowly begins to discover his pictures, all created in some kind of trance, have a way of seeing truths or affecting the future.

It's possible to say Duma Key is an example of Stephen King simply dolling up an old idea in modern clothing, relying on readers not to recall The Dead Zone. But this would be unfair in some ways. Although the similarities between this book and The Dead Zone are obvious (men injured in accidents come back with extra powers to go along with their injuries), the two differ in very noticeable ways.

First of all, King gets into his character's mind in a way he would never have been able to before his own accident. His journey into the mind of Edgar Freemantle is wonderfully realistic and emotive. Also, Freemantle, unlike Johnny Smith, welcomes his powers. He wants to paint the future, to attempt to bend events to his purposes (such as saving the life of his best friend).

The book is also very slow-paced--often too slow-paced. There just isn't enough action to justify its nearly six hundred pages. At times, the reader may even feel that King is writing words just for the sake of writing words, without the words ever getting to the crux of what's going on. Some more detail on the big bad, for one thing, would have been good.

King has lost none of his ability to write the most rounded and compelling characters, though. In addition to Freemantle, King has populated this world with very real people, who have the kinds of quirks and problems we all have. Wireman is deeply flawed as he tries to find purpose in his new post-suicide attempt life; he seeks redemption by caring for the elderly Elizabeth Eastlake, caught in her own battle against Alzheimer's. Add Freemantle's family--his two very different daughters and ex-wife--his ex-employees, and doctors, and you have a very rich cast.

But the novel just doesn't deliver fully on its promise. The Stephen King of today has crafted a good novel, when thirty years ago he would have taken this idea and created a killer read.

$18.48; hardcover; Amazon

FIRES RISING, Michael Laimo
Review by I.E. Lester

St. Peter's Church in Manhattan is a construction site - the old church being pulled down to allow a new building to be erected on the site. Nothing too unusual there I guess, but St. Peter's guards a demon - locked away in a crate under the stone floor. And the builders have just set it free.

Since the church's closure prior to the building works it had become a home to many of New York's homeless, sheltering inside its walls. But now the demon has risen these vagrants together with the church priest and the altar boy need to make a stand and defeat the demon.

Okay the plot set up might sound a little too obvious. Add to this his cast of characters is, at a glance, hackneyed - cobbled together from many other books and films. And to cap it all its good versus evil plot of disillusioned Christians fighting demons could be considered a little too familiar, something we've seen many times before. It brought to mind the kinds of horror novels that were commonplace thirty or forty years ago or more - Dennis Wheatley anyone?

But, despite these factors, Laimo has delivered a reasonable book, if not a brilliant one. It has all the right gory moments, some downright unpleasant gooey bits, and a real touch of suspense.

He has a concise way of bringing his characters to life. He puts flesh on their bones without having to spend 200 pages setting up before any action begins. And he makes you feel for them. You really want his hero-from-the-gutter types to overcome the odds.

And crucially this means he doesn't make you wait for the action, something that is most definitely a good thing for the book. Spread the story out any more and you might notice the lack of originality more.

This is old-school horror - it's like going back in time to an age before some of the touchy-feely, politically correct, "let's consider the feelings of the supernatural beings, try to understand the demon's point-of-view" horror. The horror here is simple and straightforward; it's evil for evil's sake.

It's unlikely to give anyone nightmares though. It's just not all that scary

$7.99; MM Paperback; Leisure

GOING BACK, Tony Richards
Review by I.E. Lester

In one respect, this book almost sounds like a science fiction collection. The fourteen stories contain time travel, an endlessly cycled day (à la Groundhog Day), and end-of-the-world predictions - but none of them are treated as sf. In mood these are very much darker and in many cases truly unsettling.

The opening story (and title piece) tells of a man whose life has been torn apart by the death of his daughter. He finally manages to find a way of "going back" to save her, but not quite with the result he wanted.

Following it, "A Place in the County" tells of one woman's desire to escape her New York apartment and life. She decorates it as though it were a house in the country - covering its windows with rural views - which start to come alive. And third, we have "Beautiful Stranger," a science-fictional take on zombies which shows how one man can succumb to his obsession.

These first three tales instantly draw you into the book, and make you want to read more of this author's work. They are not your normal horror - don't expect ghouls and demons to come after you wanting to eat your brains. Richards' intention is to unnerve. He manages it.

"What Malcolm Did the Day before Tomorrow" has the eponymous character encounter a stranger, who gives him the secret of reliving a day over and over and making it better, but with a really scary disturbing consequence. "The Cure" has a faith healer offering a cure that actually works, only you really wouldn't want it. "A Matter of Avoiding Crowds" plays on the fears many of us have - of being unnoticed and anonymous in a large city.

These tales give a great indication of exactly how good a writer Tony Richards is, and this is only after six of the fourteen stories. Completing the book are invisible cats with a very real effect; a man who fades away and then finally wants to make contact; two middle-aged divorced people attempting to find their way back into a relationship; a bizarre future when everyone has cosmetic surgery; wild sexual encounters with consequences; paintings that induce comas; a possessive lesbian relationship; and the end of the world.

It's a total cornucopia of unease. Richards makes his characters very much down to Earth, flawed and familiar. He connects them with the reader superbly, utilising the kinds of motivations we all have to introduce a sense of hope- -before ripping it away. These are compelling. If this author can make the transition to novels successfully, then he is likely to be one of the top names in horror in the years to come. But for now - just settle back and enjoy his skill as a short story author. Great stuff!

$12.95; Trade PB; Horror Mall

DALTON QUAYLE RIDES OUT, Paul Kane
Review by I.E. Lester

In these two short novellas, Dalton Quayle (read: a skewed Sherlock Holmes) and Humphrey Pemberton (a Dr. Watson-ish figure) set out to uncover dastardly goings-on in true melodramatic Victorian manner.

Story One sees the two against a deadly threat from under the oceans - a bit like a Cthulhu version of Jules Verne's 20,000 Leagues under the Sea, but with liberal doses of real ale thrown in. Story Two sees the pair start in Chinatown, before they encounter a dinosaur in the American Wild West. More detail about the plots than this is unnecessary.

These stories aren't about depth of plot detail or rich characters. Plots here merely serve as vehicles to allow the author's tomfoolery and jolly-japery style of humour to surface.

This book is mad - quite, quite mad. It's H.P. Lovecraft: the Carry-On, Monty Python does horror, etc. Basically what you get here are equal measures of innuendo, over-the-top-demons-style horror, basic smut, Sherlock Holmes, and surreal humour with so many film references thrown into the mix it is untrue.

Occasionally it verges on too much - the endless gags and wisecracks coming so fast and furious, you may have to come up for air from time to time. But Kane is not lambasting these cultural standards remorselessly just to gain cheap gags (even if many of his gags are very cheap). He shows himself to be a great fan of Conan Doyle, Verne, Lovecraft et al., and cinema.

His characters, although somewhat twisted, are recognisably similar to their originals - and they act accordingly. Quayle and Pemberton are Victorians, so they have Victorian outlooks. When they encounter the Chinese characters in the second tale, for instance, Pemberton is gloriously pompous and politically incorrect - showing all the "true" mastery of foreign languages and culture the British have such a great reputation for (then and now).

What defines this pair as different from the crime-fighting duo of Conan Doyle's stories is that Quayle's cases are supernaturally weird. They are also oftentimes stupid, as well as crammed to the gills with bizarre effigies of icons of modern cultures (Captains Birdseye, Ahab, and Nemo are all parodied, as are Esther Williams, Fu Manchu, Butch Cassidy & the Sundance Kid, and many others).

Furthermore, these are not exactly what you would call highbrow comic portrayals; if I said Moby Dick has become Dopey Mick, you might get the idea here. Kane is not trying to be clever; there is no biting satire, no cunning repartee. He is trying to entertain and he does. He is trying to make you laugh and groan - both of which he achieves regularly and in equal measure.

Thankfully, Kane also has the good sense to keep these stories short. It's possible that no one would be able to read a 300-page novel that maintains this pace throughout. At 71 and 62 pages, though, they are ideal: just long enough to have the stories contain more than just gags, but short enough to be readable. An ideal distraction between weightier volumes!

HORRORS BEYOND 2: STORIES OF STRANGE CREATIONS,
Edited by William Jones
Review by Chris Welch

Elder Signs Press' *Horrors Beyond 2: Stories of Strange Creations* is the sequel volume to its previously published anthology, *Horrors Beyond: Stories of Strange Realities.*

Both books are edited by William Jones. The theme of the first anthology was the relationship between technology and horror:; that sometimes advances in technology have unforeseen terrors and dark revelations connected to them.

Horrors Beyond 2 continues that theme, but takes it one step farther — not only does knowledge bring forth possible horrors, but there are menacing devices and other sinister creations (technology-based or not) out there exist that we will never understand in the first place.

The 21 stories Jones selected for this book are multi-genre, ranging from dark fantasy, dark science- fiction, Lovecraftian horror, apocalyptic end-times, to the outright surreal. Some stories mix more than one of those elements together.

All the stories in this anthology fit the theme — or oin this case, the extension of the theme — and this anthology is overall a worthy follow-up to its predecessor.

Some of the highlights of this book are Lucien Soulban's "Serenade," in which a code-breaker is given a test involving a mysterious language; Richard Lupoff's "Wyshes.com," is about making contact with aliens through mental transference; "The Margins" by Robert Weinberg, which takes a new angle on certain hounds from the Cthulhu Mythos; Tim Curran's "Wormwood" which reveals something has either entered into or grew grown within the area around Chernobyl; "The Clockmaker's Daughter," by E. Sedia, is a dark fantasy about abandonment; and Paul Melniczek's "Predicting Perdition," which is about the growing despair and memory loss of a small town.

However, the standout stories in Horrors Beyond 2 are John Shirley's "Isolation Point, California," which is about seeking human touch in a world that has been ravaged by a disease that turns people into crazed lunatics if they become too close to one another; "The Ghost Lens" by Stephen Mark Rainey, in which a mysterious artifact reveals more about nature than it should; "When the Ship Came," by John Sunseri, deals with the reaction to aliens landing more than the aliens themselves; "Spheres of Influence," by Ron Shiflet, is about family tragedy and odd metallic balls that fall from the sky; and Jay Caselberg's "Magic Fingers," which is a techno-horror story about direct-to-the-brain downloads --and simultaneously a sociological horror story about advertising.

With 21 different authors, Horrors Beyond 2 editor William Jones presents a myriad of different styles and voices for fans of dark fiction. Like its predecessor, this anthology is worth seeking out.

$15.95; TPB; Elder Signs Press

A WAGER OF BLOOD, J. W. Coffey
Review by Shawn Oetzel

J. W. Coffey's newest writing endeavor, *A Wager of Blood*, is a mixture of the paranormal, murder, and romance in a similar vein to Nora Roberts. *A Wager of Blood* does have moments where it ventures to more of the horror genre, but overall it works as a suspense thriller.

The story is focused around the Thornton Inn, a quaint restaurant in New Hampshire with a sordid past. Originally owned by the Harper family, namely Matthew Harper, in the 1700's, it was swindled away by Newell Thornton through subterfuge and a little help from the Underworld. Through the years the Inn has earned a reputation of being haunted, as guests have a nasty habit of disappearing.

Flash forward several hundred years, and the Inn is still in the possession of the Thornton family, now managed by Zach Harper--the great-nephew (many times over) of Matthew Harper. When Zach's wife Meg and her friend Frankie experience the hauntings first-hand--Frankie actually disappearing--it becomes apparent that the spirit calling the Inn home has become active once again. Zach Harper must face his own personal demons from his past if he going to save his wife and friends, along with righting a centuries-old wrong.

Ms. Coffey does a good job developing the backstory for A Wager of Blood. I enjoyed her descriptive style, which helped me picture the New Hampshire countryside as well as experience the old-world atmosphere and charm of the Thornton Inn. That said, I did have some issues with the dialogue; I found it to be unbelievable at times. The way the four main characters spoke to each other was a little too syrupy for my liking. Also, in a scene where a couple of the characters are interrogated by the police, the dialogue was simply unrealistic in my opinion.

There were also some minor plot holes, which ended up being a distraction. For example, in the scene where Frankie disappears into some paranormal void, Meg goes downstairs and gets into an argument with her husband rather than freak out. The police come in and interrogate the characters, and no one really seems to care Frankie has disappeared. Another instance is when Ms. Coffey explains that Zach Harper tries to get a $500,000 loan to buy back the Inn, but is thwarted by the Thorntons and their demon Master. However, why would he get a loan if the Inn was not for sale in the first place? This is never really explained. As I mentioned earlier, however, these are minor details and were more of a distraction than anything else.

A Wager of Blood is an entertaining read that kept me interested. Ms. Coffey did a good job of wrapping the story up, but did leave it open-ended enough as to make me believe that this not the last we have heard of Zach Harper and friends. Any fan of the thriller genre will have a fairly good time exploring Ms. Coffey's creation, the Thornton Inn, in her new novel A Wager of Blood.

$11.66; TPB; Amazon

Shroud is interested in reviewing published works of dark speculative fiction.

Please send advance review copies at least one month before publication date, accompanied by appropriate press materials. Shroud is also available for jacket blurbs provided that the content is sent well-enough in advance.

Other books can be sent at any time with the understanding that we cannot gaurantee that we will review everything and review materials cannot be returned. Sorry!

Send review materials (books, DVDs, Games, CDs) to:

Shroud Publishing
121 Mason Rd.
Milton, NH 03851

Questions? editor@shroudmagazine.com

I.E. Lester: Horror in the Flesh:

The Blood Lust of Countess Elizabeth Báthory

Many horror fans probably recognize the name Elizabeth Báthory. Most likely this is due to the 1970s cult movie Countess Dracula, which featured Ingrid Pitt as an Eastern European noblewoman who discovers that the secret of eternal life lies in regular baths in the blood of virginal young ladies. As for Elizabeth Báthory actually existing and whether the film was based on fact or merely imagination, the exact truth might not be quite what one would expect.

Elizabeth Báthory did indeed exist, although as Báthory Erzsébet (pronounced BAAH-tory air-ZHAY-bet). In Hungary, then and now, surnames are given first; Erzsébet is the Hungarian equivalent of Elizabeth. Although the film was only loosely based on Elizabeth, it did not portray her unfairly - she was, in reality, a monster.

Elizabeth was born in 1560 at Ecsed (now known as Nagyesced, near the Romanian border) to Baron George (Hungarian Gyrögy, pronounced dji-ER-dji) and Baroness Anna--two members of the same extended noble family, as was the custom of the time. Her family was notorious and influential. One uncle was an alchemist and known devil-worshipper; another, Stephen (Štefan), would later become the King of Poland. An aunt, Klara, was even reputed to be a witch who enjoyed torturing her servants.

Báthory was born during turbulent times. Hungary was in a state of near-constant war with the Turks, and large areas of the country were under Turkish occupation - including the twin cities of Buda and Pest, which form the modern-day Hungarian capital. During Elizabeth's childhood, however, a truce had been brokered between the Holy Roman Emperor and the Ottoman Turks, allowing Báthory to enjoy relative peace during her early years.

Elizabeth was a gifted child and was given a broad education. She became fluent and literate in Hungarian, Latin and German during an era when most Hungarian nobles could not read or write to any great degree, and women were generally not educated at all.

At the age of eleven, Elizabeth became engaged to sixteen-year-old Count Ferenc (pronounced FAIR-ents) Nadasdy, an athletic type who was poor at scholarly pursuits. This was not a love-match, but rather a union arranged by Ferenc's mother Ursula in order to gain political influence. As the marriage was not Elizabeth's choice, she had little problem violating her relationship with Ferenc, both before and during their marriage. Indeed, prior to the wedding, she became pregnant by a peasant from the village and bore a daughter. The child would be sequestered to prevent embarrassment to the family.

Elizabeth and Ferenc married on May 8, 1575. It was a lavish affair with many guests in attendance. Holy Roman Emperor Maximillian II had been invited, although he declined to attend, unwilling to risk travelling long distances during such a dangerous time. Ferenc would add the more prestigious Báthory to his surname, while Elizabeth elected to keep her birth name intact.

Through this marriage, Elizabeth became mistress of Castle Sarvar (SHAR-var), as well as of the Nadasdy estates. Although different in many ways, Elizabeth and Ferenc both shared a reputation for cruelty. Their punishments involved regular beatings for servants, as well as pushing pins into the lips, and under the fingernails, of servant girls. Servants accused of theft were stripped and had heated coins pressed into their flesh; one girl who chattered too much for Elizabeth's liking had her lips sewn together.

The most severe punishments the couple inflicted included stripping a serving girl naked outdoors in the winter snows and pouring cold water over her until she died. They covered another's naked body in honey, then left her tied down so bugs, bees and wild animals would slowly devour her.

Typical of the nobility of the time, Ferenc was a career soldier. He would become a famous war-hero, one of five heroes known as "The Unholy Quintet" who would instil terror in the Turks. The Turks even gave him a nickname - "The Black Knight of Hungary." His soldiering kept him away from his home for lengthy periods, causing a delay of ten years before their union produced children. (The marriage would eventually produce four children, Anna, Ursula, Katherina and Paul, to whom Elizabeth would prove a devoted and protective mother.) Elizabeth was certainly not celibate during her husband's absences. She took many lovers, male and female, and frequently visited her aunt Klara, who lived an openly bisexual life and always kept large numbers of available

attractive young women in her home. At one point, Elizabeth even ran away with one of her lovers, later returning to be forgiven by Ferenc.

Things for Elizabeth changed in 1604. Ferenc took ill and died. After a very short--bordering on scandalously short--period of mourning lasting just four weeks, Elizabeth left Castle Sarvar to spend her time between the Royal Court in Vienna and her castle in Cachtice (pronounced CHAKH-tee-tsay), located in the country's northwest of the country (now situated in Slovakia).

Ferenc's death has been cited by many as a turning point for Elizabeth, a trigger for her more extreme practices. This event should not be seen as such, however; it is very apparent that her sadistic behaviour was already well established.

Another common belief about Elizabeth is that she bathed in blood. No evidence exists of whether she actually did so. It is well known is that Báthory was a vain woman, worried about age fading her beauty. Rumours have suggested that one day a young servant girl accidentally pulled Elizabeth's hair whilst combing it. The Countess reacted by instantly slapping the girl's face, drawing blood. Some of the blood spilled onto Báthory's hand, whereafter she noticed that her skin had become more youthful; she subsequently began to bathe regularly in the blood of servant girls.

There are absolutely no contemporary accounts of such bathing though, and this story seems to have appeared only in the 18th century. What is substantiated, though, is that there are many accounts of torture sessions that would leave Elizabeth totally covered in the blood of her victims. If indeed Báthory never actually bathed herself in blood, this could well be the origin of this element of her legend.

She is known to have escalated her activities upon moving to Cachtice. Partly this is due to the arrival of a mysterious woman named Anna Darvulia, soon after Elizabeth's own move. Darvulia is said to have become a sort of torture tutor, teaching Elizabeth many new methods of inflicting pain.

Other helpers joined her also

- the manservant known only as "Ficzko" (the Hungarian word for "lad," pronounced FITZ-ko with a short "o"); her children's wet nurse Illona Jó; a peasant woman named Dorothea Szentes (SENT-esh); and a washerwoman named Katarina Beneczky (be-NETS-kee).

Over the next five years, Báthory and her entourage committed countless atrocities. Later testimony from one of her accomplices described one torture session as including a number of naked young women laid flat on the floor of her bedroom, tortured to such an extent that the whole floor was awash with blood. Another account reported a twelve-year-old girl, who was retrieved following an escape from the castle, then placed in a tiny cage with dozens of tiny knives protruding inwards--and shaken so that the girl was sliced apart.

Elizabeth did, however, consider her victims to be somewhat human, and even went as far as ensuring that many of the girls received proper Christian burial. At least, she did at first. As the killings increased, the local priests refused to go along with her activities, stopped co-operating with her, and attempted to raise awareness of these murders.

Her behaviour went unnoticed (or maybe just ignored) for years by the rulers of the day. However, the freedom to commit her crimes was not to last forever. Elizabeth's behaviour changed when Anna Darvulia died following a stroke and Erzsi Majorova (AIR-zhee MAH-jor-ova) replaced her. Darvulia had increased Báthory's sadistic range, but she had also ensured that only peasant serving girls were abused. Majorova seemed to loose any remaining shackles.

Báthory began taking the daughters of minor noble houses as victims, and also stopped using discretion in the means of corpse disposal. One report depicts her servants throwing the bodies of four murdered girls from her castle's ramparts in full view of the villagers.

Taking noble-born victims could not go unnoticed, and the King of Hungary ordered Count Thurzo (TOOR-zho) to arrest her. Thurzo was Elizabeth's cousin and wanted to spare the family the embarrassment this scandal could cause. He decided to circumvent the need for a trial and pronounced her guilty, sentencing her to live out her life imprisoned within a bricked-up room in her castle at Cachtice. His pronouncement declared she was "like a wild animal" and that she was to "disappear from this world and never reappear in it again."

Evidence suggests that politics played an important part in Báthory's downfall. During his 25 years of soldiering, Ferenc had earned a considerable wage due from the King of Hungary. This was not fully paid, and even though Ferenc was dead, Elizabeth did not consider the King's debt to have died with him. In addition to her sadistic behaviours, Báthory had determinedly petitioned the King for payment in full.

Báthory remained holed up in her prison for over three years until she was discovered lying dead, face down in the middle of her cell on August 21, 1614. The local residents found abhorrent the idea of the body of such a monster being interred in hallowed ground in their village, and objected to plans to bury her in Cachtice. Although the nobility could have insisted, Thurzo did not want the likely desecration of her grave to further sully the family name. Her body was instead transported to Ecsed, the original seat of the Báthory family, where she was buried at the place of her birth.

Her accomplices were not as fortunate. Illona Jó and Dorothea Szentes suffered having their fingers cut off with red-hot pincers before being thrown alive onto a fire. Ficzko was spared the extremes of this sentence due to his youth, and was merely decapitated. Erzsi Majorova would also be executed. Only Beneczky would be spared from death, after a plea of mercy made by a witness at her trial.

Some have suggested that Elizabeth was insane, having suffered seizures throughout childhood, possibly as a result of epilepsy. Also suggested as a factor are the speculated effects of the inbreeding rife in Hungarian noble families of the day. The noble-born considered themselves far removed from common folk, whom they viewed less important than livestock; hence the preference for marrying within their own limited gene pool.

Insanity seems unlikely, however. Elizabeth wrote many letters in connection with her position; none showed evidence of her being deranged - and no contemporary account mentions insanity.

Elizabeth also wrote a detailed diary of her acts, even going as far as complaining when a victim died quickly without having endured much torture. She stated, "She was too small." In this diary, Báthory listed more than 600 victims.

Beyond doubt, Elizabeth was cruel, and yet to her own children, she was a doting parent. This seems an apparent contradiction, but we must remember the times she lived in were vastly removed from today in terms of morality. Mass murder was an accepted method of controlling a population, and a frequent tactic used in warfare. Elizabeth Báthory went above and beyond this, however, and took cruelty to a new level. If her exploits had reached a wider audience at the time, it is possible we may be talking of bathoryism rather than sadism.

It has been suggested that Báthory is part of the inspiration for Bram Stoker's character Dracula. Stoker based Dracula on Vlad Tepes ("The Impaler"). Tepes, in reality, was a devout Christian warrior, even if extreme in battle savagery. He was a Romanian, a prince of Wallachia; Dracula was a Hungarian count. Dracula drinks the blood of his victims, which then rejuvenates him--something never attributed to Tepes, but rather similar to the legend of Countess Báthory. However, Stoker made no mention of Elizabeth in the detailed research notes he made before writing Dracula, so it cannot be said for sure whether he adapted parts of her life for his novel.

Báthory was a monster, displaying a total disregard for human life. She may or may not have been the madwoman who bathed in blood, but, regardless, was a very disturbed person. If we believe she was insane, then we could attach her actions to this madness; but if she was sane, then we have to accept she was truly evil.

∞∞∞∞

I.E. Lester is a lifelong fan of science fiction and horror. A school trip to a Jacobean Mansion and spooky tales of ghostly inhabitants launched a fascination with supernatural horror, although not a belief in the reality (he is still a strong skeptic). A washed-out family holiday confirmed his fate when the cover of an Isaac Asimov collection attracted a nine-year-old eye. He has spent the subsequent three decades amassing a large library featuring the works of King, Bradbury, Heinlein, Clarke, Lovcraft, Poe and many, many others. He studied Mathematics and Astrophysics whilst at University and works as a software designer. When not reading sf, horror, history or factual science, he can often be found watching cricket or rugby, or wandering medieval streets in France or Italy.

Ankle-Biters
By Christa M. Miller

The party had gone well until the biting started.

Patsy would never say it out loud, but of course it was the Mexican kid who started it. His size made him look like he was going on five, not three; his mother barely spoke English, but everyone could tell by the tone she used with him, that she let him get away with murder. Wandering into the woods behind the house, for instance.

It was a sullen, mean-tempered day, the sky a dull hazy white. The heavy moisture had sapped everyone's energy; the adults clustered around the tables of wilting food on the deck, while the kids wandered the yard. The day hadn't even allowed enough sun or warmth to play with the water toys. They sat on the grass in a heap that reminded Patsy of something from a crime-scene photo. So all the kids were bored and whiny, and they'd started to get inventive. Patsy guessed that was why Eladio took off.

No one knew anything about it until Araceli approached, eyes teary and bugged out, chest heaving. Patsy's friend Andrea, who'd minored in Spanish, had to translate the woman's rapid panicky speech. "Eladio went for a walk? Walked off. She's been calling for him and he won't answer. She thinks something happened to him in the forest."

Patsy did her best to suppress her irritation. The trees behind their property were woods, not forest; they bordered another development of family homes. At their deepest point was a murky slimy frog pond, but the only thing that lived there was--

Jesus. He could've fallen in. "Someone find Chad." He's probably inside feeding his face. "Jason? Honey, take some of the other dads and go back by the frog pond. Eladio might've--"

Araceli screamed, but it was a cry of relief rather than fear or anger. Patsy turned to look behind her. Sure enough, Eladio had appeared at the property boundary. But something was wrong. His eyes were blank, his skin pale. Before Patsy could stop her, Araceli rushed him, arms outstretched, mouth moving as she seemed to unleash every Spanish word ever spoken.

It stopped the moment Eladio bit her. Everyone stared. Patsy thought she heard a few snickers, like the other parents thought Araceli had finally gotten her due. Then Araceli screamed. It was high, ululating. Unnatural, though Patsy couldn't say why. Chills raced down her body.

Jason and his dad rushed to help Araceli. At first they tried to pull her away from her son, but he held on tight, the skin pulling so taut Patsy thought he'd take a chunk out of Araceli's arm. Finally her father-in-law pried the kid's mouth off his mother's arm like a dog off a shoe. Eladio had drawn blood.

The boy snapped at Jason's dad, who hauled off and smacked Eladio so hard that the kid fell on his rear end. Was that necessary? she wanted to holler, but Jason and his dad were hustling Araceli across the lawn like they were running from Eladio.

Araceli's husband Chad appeared, chowing down on a brownie from one of the dessert plates. Patsy hadn't planned to serve dessert for another hour. "What happened?" Chad sounded genuinely confused. He blinked at his wife, the two men flanking her.

Patsy told him. By then Araceli had reached him. He looked at her arm. "Hospital," he managed to say before he threw up the brownie, along with the cheese and crackers, veggies with dip,

Shroud #2 March/April

and burger he'd consumed that afternoon.

Patsy looked too, and nearly had the same reaction. She'd never seen gangrene, and she knew it couldn't set in that fast, but it was her first thought when she saw Araceli's wound.

"We'll watch Eladio," Patsy heard her father-in-law say.

Chad nodded as he led Araceli out the door. Patsy felt sorry for him then. For both of them. She thought it was good of her father-in-law to make up for hitting the kid. Then she heard him murmur to Jason, "For God's sake, find that kid. Tie him up, knock him out if you have to. But find him and get him the hell to a hospital."

As if in response, one of the moms spoke. "He looks okay now." But she wasn't looking at Jason's dad, or even at Eladio. Instead she studied her manicure.

Patsy glanced at Eladio. He'd gotten off the ground without so much as a whimper. Strange. And she couldn't say she agreed with the other mother. Eladio looked more gray than pale now, and his stare was blanker than it had been.

Still, he wasn't behaving that differently. From what Patsy could tell, he hummed to himself as he wandered. "God help that kid if he's autistic," the woman remarked to Andrea. "His mother'd probably want him exorcised."

Patsy opened her mouth to chastise her, then shut it. She was probably right. Still, she wondered if the boy missed his mother, if he was scared. "Eladio!" she called.

He stopped. Stared up at her on the porch, eyes locked on hers. He took a few steps toward her. Patsy realized she wanted to scream and run, but she could do neither. It was as if he'd mesmerized her.

Then his gaze shifted to something else, and he changed direction. Following Friday, the cat from next door. As Patsy watched, Friday hissed at Eladio. Then it ran into the tangle of blackberry bushes between the properties. Eladio climbed in after it. If the prickers scratched him, he didn't react.

Two other kids ran after him before she could stop them. Why should she want to do that? She shook herself, turned to go down the deck steps. May as well take the food back inside. No one had eaten since Chad's episode.

"Mooooom!" came a wail just as she reached the lawn.

Now what? Patsy thought. At least that wasn't her kid.

It was his best friend. Brandan. Andrea's son. Tearing around the corner, sobbing. Brandan had followed Eladio. Had he been bitten too?

Andrea sprang down the deck steps to tend to him. From this distance, Patsy couldn't tell whether he was hurt. She looked around the yard for Kyle. Hoped he didn't feel gypped by so much dysfunction at his birthday party. She didn't see him.

Andrea scooped Brandan up and came toward Patsy. "I think we'll be going now."

"What's wrong? Was he--is he okay?" Patsy couldn't bring herself to say the word "bitten." Brandan mumbled something into his mother's neck. It sounded like "eating the cat." But that couldn't be right, it was just Patsy's brain making connections based on what she'd seen.

Andrea gave her a final, troubled look. Then she turned and fled into the house.

Another mother, Ginny, came up to Patsy. She, too, looked nervous. "Have you seen Zach?"

Zach. The other kid who'd followed Eladio. "No." Patsy glanced into the yard, as if the kids were about to mount a water-balloon attack on the adults. "Did you look in the house?"

The relief in Ginny's face wasn't genuine. Patsy could tell by the way her frown deepened around her smile. She bet Ginny had already checked in the house, maybe hoped she'd missed Zach somehow.

After Ginny had gone, Patsy looked around the yard. For all of today's weirdness, it certainly looked like a normal toddler birthday party. Adults talked over plates of half-eaten food, paid minimal attention to the kids who played in the rest of the yard. The worst part about suburban culture: the adults tended to rely on each other to babysit, taking responsibility only when they had to comfort tears away. Otherwise, no one was in charge.

Then Patsy realized it was worse than she thought. The only kid playing in the rest of the yard was Kyle, alone in the sandbox.

For Christ's sake. His birthday, and no one was playing with him. Where the hell were they all? Why had she invited Eladio, who had clearly started this whole thing? Because she felt sorry for immigrant Araceli, that was why.

She spotted Zach, heading across the yard toward Kyle. That was good, that was all right. She had to find Ginny, let her know. As she turned to go into the house, two other kids came out of the trees. Both stumbled toward the sandbox.

She found Ginny coming out of the bathroom. Moisture glistened on the other woman's brow; she must have thrown some water on her face. Patsy smiled at her. "I found Zach. He's in the yard."

Ginny relaxed. "Thank goodness. Patsy, I hate to say it, but I think we'll just go home now."

"Sure, I understand." Patsy did--and didn't. Yes, the thing with Eladio had been disturbing. But did it have to ruin the whole party, especially now that Araceli had been taken care of?

Ginny followed her. They made it as far as the deck before Patsy halted. Again she wanted to run, but couldn't say why. She just found it odd that 2- and 3-year-olds, who when they'd arrived had run all over the yard and only played "together" in that they used the same swing set or toy, now clustered together in the sandbox. They reminded Patsy of 8-year-olds frying ants with a magnifying glass; they hadn't even clustered around the piñata's sweet guts with the same intensity. In fact, they'd hardly seemed interested in the candy.

Patsy began to walk toward the children. She couldn't see Kyle. She wanted to make sure everything was all right, especially with no one really watching the kids.

She barely recognized Zach when his little gray face popped up. It was smeared with something dark, like mud, except he was in the sandbox, and there was no water in sight.

Closer now, she saw what the kids had clustered around: another child lay in the sand. She recognized Kyle's Thomas the Tank Engine sneakers. Prone. She started to run for him.

Zach saw her--and screamed. He sounded like Araceli.
The others' heads jerked up. She looked from one small face to the next. Their mouths were stained dark like Zach's, some stained brighter red--

She looked into the sandbox. The dark stains were all over Kyle, too. So were his intestines. Her throat worked on a scream, but before she could release it, she felt the teeth. Needle-like teeth, the kind she'd felt at her breast just before she weaned Kyle last spring.

The last thing she did, after Zach tore the chunk from her calf, was to fall forward into the children's grasping hands.

∞∞∞∞

Christa M. Miller, a resident of northern New England, tries to avoid children's birthday parties as much as she possibly can. Failing that, she is contemplating a "Living Dead" theme for her own son's 5th birthday. Read more of her fiction at her website, http://www.christammiller.com.

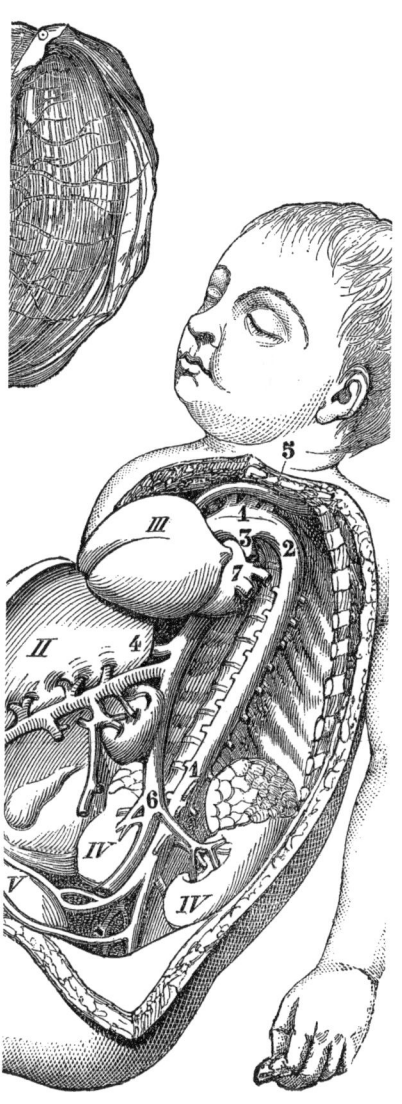

Snow: MySpace Flash Fiction Contest #1

1st MySpace Flash Fiction Contest #1
"Snow"

Shroud recently relocated from Nevada to New Hampshire (our home State) after totally and completely failing to adapt to the strip malls and stucco of Spanish Springs. We were successful in locating a rustic log home on more than five acres of land that features old stone walls, White Birch trees, and access to 100s of acres of forest land. It's really quite beautiful. In addition, it is also quite eerie—especially at night when the woods surrounding the house go still and quiet, and our fertile imaginations conjure up stalking beasts and arcane shadows.

After record snowfalls this winter, I awoke on several occasions to find a fresh blanket of snow surrounding the house and burdening the trees. At these times the silence was dramatic as the snow muffled all sound. Such beauty opens the mind to a world of fantastic possibilities, especially the dark kind. Therefore I had an idea. What if I shared these images with my MySpace friends and gave them the opportunity to offer their creative vision to me in 500 words or less. The response was outstanding. More than 75 writers pitched their stories to me and succeeded in scaring my pants off. I am now unable to venture into my back yard.

I was the sole judge of the entries so take that for what its worth. I selected the following winner and honorable mentions based upon the mood and feeling that they evoked; the writing style and clarity; and the ability to effectively capture the supplied images (facing page) in words. I know you are going to enjoy these nasty little tales as much as I did. Oh, by the way, we will be launching the second MySpace Flash Fiction Contest very soon, so go to www.myspace.com/shroudmag and become our friend!

-Tim

Winner:

Title: The White
Author: Saranna Dewylde
MySpace ID: Saranna

She'd been buried alive.

But it wasn't so horrible a fate, because Constance actually was dead. She'd died out there, thrashing and screaming, her body moving through that rolling desert of white, the convulsions of flesh a mockery of snow angels.

The heat of her life had poured from her eyes, her mouth, had dripped like manna down beneath the snow, revealing the rust-colored ground beneath, the marker of all those who had bled before, those who had stained this cursed place.

Her mama and papa were propped against the far wall. Their dark eye sockets saw everything, yet their crimson mouths bespoke nothing. Their righteousness was silent and still.

She was so hungry. Sharp pains were knives through her belly, through that emptiness that seemed to engulf her. Connie knew she shouldn't be hungry, after all, she'd left all of her red out there in the white nothing. She shivered, only feeling the cold on her forearms, in those gashes from wrist to elbow where the fascia hung like a curtain at a peep show.

Connie laid her head on Mama's breast, the hard marble of dead flesh no longer a concern. She hummed a lullaby, the one her mama had always used when she was scared. Connie held Mama's hand, petted the slender white fingers that had always soothed her.

"No one is coming, baby."

Constance continued to hum and pet Mama. She looked to Papa, with the stern tilt to his head, the age spots on the backs of his hands that were erupting into boils where the last of his red was surging to find the white.

"His fault, precious. Leave him. But take me. I'll be with you always."

She moved to take the family Bible from her papa's melting lap, but she howled when it singed her fingers. Connie wanted the cold now, the white. She was unafraid; it would soothe her, hide her, love her.

Connie brought her mother's pristine fingers to her mouth, where she kissed them each so softly, rubbed them past her lips, touched her tongue to each tip before letting her razor-sharp predator's teeth find the last of the red.

Later, out in the veil, the frigid nothing: a girl in a white dress danced amidst the snowflakes, singing a lullaby her mama brought with her from the old country.

And her ballerina slippers left no tracks in that cosmetic white powder.

Copyright 2008 Saranna Dewylde

Runner up

Title: Crunch
Author: R. Scott McCoy
MySpace ID: Necrotic Tissue

Christopher sat on his bed and stared at the falling snow that drifted over the edge of the deck. He pulled his Star Wars comforter to his face and screamed into the Millennium Falcon. He'd always known that if he told his parents what was happening, they would also die.

Even sitting up in bed, Christopher could feel the crunching vibrate through his bones. It got louder when he lay down, and he could always hear the heavy crunch of footsteps in winter.

It started when he was six. He woke from a nightmare and could just make out the sound of heavy steps in the fresh snow. Even then, he knew it wasn't possible to hear footsteps at the North Pole, but in his dreams, he felt more than saw a hazy force striding toward him through the swirling wastes.

There was a hint of eyes in the tempest, dark and malevolent. Hours after he woke, he could still feel the ancient, clawing hunger of the thing.

Each year it came closer, and each year he was saved by the spring thaw. At the end of the last winter, he could hear the heavy footfalls only miles to the North. He'd stayed up all night, waiting for death. In the morning, the sun broke through the overcast, the icicles started to drip, and the crunching steps faded once again.

There would be no reprieve this year. The groundhog had predicted six more weeks of winter, and despite the calendar's insistences that it was April 2nd, the spring showers were heavy and white. There would be no flowers.

He waited for next step, as inevitable as the death it heralded.

It didn't fall, and the silence stretched from seconds to minutes. For the first time since the last thaw, Christopher dared to hope. The sky had grown lighter, and he was sure the creature couldn't travel during the day.

His hope surged as he broke free from his covers and ran to the window, searching the barren landscape.

If he made it until morning, he could run away. Hitch a ride like in the movies, or use his allowance for a bus ticket. Maybe check out Disney World. He could be a hundred miles south before sunset. When the thaw came, he would come home.

He searched between the thick branches where he and his friends played. The shadows shrunk before the light, and his smile fell away.

Christopher looked directly into the eyes of ancient, hungry evil. The wave of cold flowed over him, freezing his tears before they could touch his cheeks. He tried to cry out, to turn and run. Before he could even shiver, his body hardened.

His last sensation was a feeling of peace as warmth swept through his body, taking away his fear and last breath as his flesh crystallized.

Hundreds of miles to the east, a small boy woke to the sound of crunching snow and screamed.

Copyright 2008 R. Scott McCoy

Runner up

Title: The Devil Calls
Author: John P. Wilson
MySpace ID: John P. Wilson

The morning was cold, wet and white. It was a bitter day, and the black spruces and pines slowly waved in the breeze.

Chad was about to open the door to his vehicle when his wife called his name.

He glanced around. Nothing was there but snow and silence.

"Sarah?"

A gust of wind slapped him across the face, and the pickup's antenna rocked back and forth. The sudden sound unnerved him. His cell phone went off. King of the Road almost made him piss his pants.

"Hello?"

"Hey, honey," his wife said.

"Hey, baby."

"How is everything?"

"It's snowed every day since I've been here."

"Figures," Sarah said.

"You know, I thought you'd decided to come up here and surprise me."

"Not a chance."

"I could have sworn I heard you calling my name. I even looked for you. No one was there."

"That's creepy, sweetheart. Momma always told me if someone calls your name and no one's around, then it's Lucifer. As long as you don't answer back, you're okay."

"That's just an old wives' tale," he said.

The cell phone died. Chad held it in his hand and stared at it. He thought about what Sarah had said. He put the cell phone in his coat pocket.

He opened the driver's door and leaned inside the cab to get the box of ammunition he'd left on the seat. He grabbed it and straightened himself.

There was a flash of movement near a pine tree.

"Hello?" he said.

Chad thought about his rifle in the corner of the living room. He thought about what he might have seen moving in the woods. He heard nothing.

Something was watching him.

Chad pumped his legs, his arms flailing, almost losing his footing in the snow as he rushed for the log cabin.

He turned to look behind him. Nothing.

He slammed the door, locked it, and then ran for his rifle. He picked it up and crept to the window. He peered outside and saw his red box of ammunition resting in the snow.

"Shit fire." He dropped the rifle on the floor.

There was a knock at the door.

Chad could feel his heart pounding. He tried to swallow.

Another knock. It sounded like a shotgun blast in the small cabin.

He inched his way to the door. There was no peephole. He felt his eyes water and fought back the urge to yell.

More knocking. Louder and more forceful.

"Leave me alone!"

Silence.

Chad waited there for almost an hour, his ears straining for sounds of movement.

He opened the door.

Nothing.

He slammed it shut and turned around.

His box of ammunition was on the floor.

"Surprise!" Sarah said. She shot him once in the head with the rifle and then dragged his body outside for the snow or wild animals.

Whichever came first.

Copyright 2008 John P. Wilson

Runner up

Title: Snowbound
Author: Brian J. Hatcher
MySpace ID: Brian J. Hatcher

Isaac couldn't feel his cellphone's earbud anymore, but he could still hear Jess's voice. "Is that the wind?" she asked. "Are you outside?"

"I talked to your Dad today."

"That isn't funny."

"He might still be inside. Wow, the snow's really coming down now."

"Have you been drinking?"

"I should be freezing, sitting on a deck chair in my robe. I'm shivering a little, but I'm not that cold. Isn't that strange?"

"You're out in your bathrobe? You'll freeze half to death."

"Not half. By morning, I should make it all the way."

"You can't be serious," Jess said. "If you don't go inside, I'll call the police."

"The roads are covered. The salt trucks can't get through, and the snow's still coming down hard. No one's going to be able to drive up here for a couple of days, at least."

"Damn it, I said get your drunk ass in the house right now!" She sounded more desperate than angry.

"Your Dad said few drinks would make it easier. He said freezing was the best way to die. He froze to death, didn't he?"

"Stop it! You didn't talk to Dad. He's dead."

"He was right. God, Jess, I wish you could see this. It's so beautiful. The trees are white and heavy with snow. Everything has a glow to it. Sometimes the moon peeks out from behind a cloud, just for a moment, and the whole world lights up. The snowflakes twinkle like stars. They're falling on my hands, and they're not melting anymore."

"Isaac, listen to me," Jess said. "I want you to get up, and go inside."

"I don't think I can stand. I've been out here too long. I can't even see my feet for all the snow."

"You have to try."

"Your father told me it was all right not to love someone anymore if they didn't love you back. I wanted to stop loving you. I did. But I can't. Even after everything that's happened, I just can't."

"Isaac, get up, please."

"I just wanted to call and let you know that it's okay that you love someone else. You don't have to worry about me getting in the way."

"Damn it, there isn't anybody else!"

"You don't have to lie, not anymore."

"I swear to God, there's no one else. Please, I'll do anything you want. Just get up."

"Doesn't matter. So, I can't make you love me. Even if I could, it wouldn't be right."

"I do love you! Oh, God, Isaac, listen to me! I love you!"

Isaac sighed, his breath no longer warm enough to fog the air. He closed his eyes. "You do. I don't know if you loved me before, or if you ever will again, but right now, this moment, you love me. And that makes me feel so-- warm."

Then, either the phone or the earbud lost power, maybe. Isaac wasn't sure. But he could still hear Jess, somehow, somewhere in the darkness.

Please.

Please…

Copyright 2008 Brian J. Hatcher

Runner up

Title: You Must Be Starving
Author: Thersa Matsuura
MySpace ID: Terrie Matsuura

"You must be starving."

The old woman draped a sour-smelling rug of animal pelt across my shoulders and patted away the melting snow from my cheek with the hem of her skirt.

I was starving, and worried sick. Early that morning I had left Mother alone. I'll collect some firewood, find something to eat. She discouraged me, reading the unfavorable sky and uneasy feeling in her stomach. But at near twelve years of age--a year older than Taro was when he started to provide for us--I wouldn't listen.

It was just us now, and Mother was weak with the Cough.

I huddled, half-frozen and exhausted, on the straw-tatami mat floor, watching the day grow dark outside. A fire warmed my back as I gazed out the window at the continuing storm. The entire landscape was enveloped in beautiful dollops of snow, which reminded me of enormous powdered rice cakes weighting down the trees, piling soft on the shed, over the fence. Rice cakes like Mother used to make on New Year's and Boy's Day.

I was starving.

My eyes stung when I thought of her back there, worried, cold, hungry. How long had I been gone? Would I be able to find my way back tonight?

"It's okay, you can stay here for the night," the old woman said as if reading my mind. I turned to see a faint grin as she hobbled across the floor towards me.

"Douzo." Blowing through the steam, she placed a lacquer bowl full of hot soup into my trembling hands. "It's the last."

I tried to refuse, but she gently insisted. It would be rude to devour such a treat in one gulp. I bowed my head.

"Itadakimasu." Inhaling the salty, nutty fragrance, I stared into the settling clouds of miso. In slow motion they disintegrated, but not around a clump of mountain grass or an odd-shaped potato as I expected. Instead, they revealed the plump bend of pink flesh torn away at the knuckle and a loose fingernail. My stomach dropped. I looked up.

"Don't worry," she laughed. I gazed into the old woman's eyes and caught a glint of crimson reflected from the fire, watched it spread through the black and splinter bloodshot through the whites. She seemed to grow taller, or maybe the room just fell away. I retched and dropped the bowl.

The hag continued her wail, a line of drool running freely from the corner of her black lips. Dark hollows caved the lines on her forehead and under her eyes as a smile cut impossibly wide across her face, stretching from ear to ear and opening two rows of crooked and brutal teeth. She gripped my shoulder with one powerful claw.

"It's the last of the soup," she said. "But tomorrow I'll feast on something fresh and young."

Copyright 2008 Terrie Matsuura

Runner up

Title: Entombed
Author: Sheldon S. Higdon
MySpace ID: Sheldon S. Higdon

The snow fell harder as Evan stood in the kitchen of his cabin, looking through the sliding glass door that led to his back deck. Usually at this time of year, he and his wife Matilda would be barbecuing, but those days were gone. He could see the birch trees in his back yard bending to the winter wind, hunched against the grey sky like pale old men. The thicket of evergreens struggled to stand erect, clinging to one another for support; even the great sentry evergreen that stood separated from the icy green pack appeared weary. No grey squirrels scampered about the frozen tundra, no crows cawed in the bitter air, and most importantly, there were no signs of human life.

Evan's neighbor, James Kimball, had left for Florida four days ago. The last of the news reports had come in three weeks ago, and since then…nothing...no information and no power. Blankets were all Evan had to keep warm. So whether Florida was the answer, no one knew. But Mr. Kimball took the chance anyway. That wasn't something Evan even considered. Setting foot outside would be an inevitable suicide; frostbite waited for those who dared. And it may have cost James Kimball his life. Even Evan's truck had succumbed to the deep cold early on, as well as his generator.

As Evan stood there, he wished he could once again see airplanes threading the blue sky with their white contrails. Blue sky, he thought. To see that again would be divine; to see the sun shining and melting the snow would be a sign of life. But now, in this everlasting winter, the only sign of life was the sound of Evan's own muted heartbeat.

White puffs exuded as his breathing became heavier. His eyes began to stick at every blink. He shivered, rubbing his mitted hands together. The layers of clothing and blankets no longer kept him warm. It was only a matter of time before he followed Matilda, who'd died yesterday, and his two cats, Keene and Ketchum, who'd died two weeks ago. All preserved in the snow, he thought--or better yet, entombed.

He had no answers to this ice age. But he remembered last year, when people marched in the streets of New York protesting the government's stance on global warming, carrying signs proclaiming that the end was near while others chanted for Al Gore to run in the next presidential race. Unfortunately, the former prevailed and indeed the end came. Maybe, Evan thought, the earth finally decided to rid itself of the vermin that polluted her with their ignorance and ego. But it was only a thought.

The sliding glass door was now covered in a thin sheet of ice, and through it Evan saw a blurry field where the evergreens seemed to huddle together and the birch trees were fading away into the snowy abyss. And even the great evergreen that stood sentry, like him, was getting ready to die.

Copyright 2008 Sheldon S. Higdon

Prize

Saranna Dewylde, our winner, receieved a free copy of the Shroud Anthology, *Beneath the Surface: 13 Shocking Tales of Terror*. In addition, she will receive paid publication in this issue of Shroud. Our runners up received publication. Please visit us on MySpace at www.myspace.com/shroud.

"Look, it's not you, it's me..."

"I just need some space right now..."

"It's just not the right time for a relationship..."

"No, there is not someone else..."

"I just think we'd be better off as friends..."

"Yes, you heard me, let's just be friends..."

www.myspace.com/shroudmag

CAN WE BE FRIENDS?

Windows to the Soul
Film and DVD Reviews

The Wickedest Man in the World:
IN SEARCH OF THE GREAT BEAST: ALEISTER CROWLEY
Review by Marie O'Regan

This past September saw the DVD release of a documentary film about the life of renowned Satanist Aleister Crowley, the Great Beast. This fascinating insight into the mind of one of last century's most infamous figures makes one wonder: why was now the right time for such a film, and what triggered its making?

Director Robert Garofalo actually first wanted to do the film in 1987, but extensive initial research brought him to the conclusion that he was "too inexperienced" to do the subject justice. Twenty years and many films later, he finally felt he had the expertise to bring Aleister Crowley's history to life.

Garofalo followed three basic rules that he applies to any project to see if Crowley was a suitable subject. First, a blind person should be able to listen to the narrative and understand the storyline; second, a deaf person should be able to watch the narrative and follow the storyline; and last, is there someone who wouldn't want this documentary shown?

The production definitely qualifies on the first two counts, and there are any number of people who wouldn't want this documentary shown. Crowley claims to have influenced Hitler, and links are shown to people such as L. Ron Hubbard, a supposed associate who went on to claim he'd "infiltrated" the Order of the Golden Dawn in order to expose it—even rescued a woman from its clutches. Hubbard, of course, went on to found the Church of Scientology. Links are also made to George W. Bush; Crowley knew his grandmother, Pauline Pierce, mother of Barbara Bush (born eight months after Pierce visited Crowley's home, the Abbey of Thalema in Cefalù, Sicily).

Joss Ackland as Narrator

Although a large portion of the film concentrates on Crowley's infamous occult activities, we also learn that he was a chess master, a highly competent mountaineer, a poet, writer, and artist—a true "renaissance man." One other thing Crowley certainly appears to have been a master of was the art of self-promotion – and it becomes immediately apparent that the film will provoke debate, and a strong response from many quarters.

Garofalo has already experienced an extreme reaction to the film in many cases. Christians have branded him "a disciple of the Antichrist," followers of Crowley's teachings have sent him curses, Scientologists have sent him subliminal threats, hackers tried to shut down the film's MySpace page…and "experts" on Crowley have tried to discredit the documentary without even having seen it. The man behind the film's musical score, Rick Wakeman, has also had to defend his position as project composer – something that seems bizarre when all he is "guilty" of doing is composing music to accompany a film, and is in fact known to be a devout Christian. It would seem, then, that Garofalo has achieved his third aim in spades.

The film charts Crowley's life from his birth as Edward Alexander Crowley on October 12, 1875 until his death in Hastings on December 1, 1947, at the age of 72. No stone appears to have been left unturned; we learn of his harsh, deeply religious childhood and schooling, his subsequent rebellion, and the start of his obses-

Thomas Bewly as Aleister Corwley

sion with all that was forbidden – leading to his realization that he was fascinated with "the enemies of heaven." We learn of his sexuality – although Crowley had many relationships with women, he also had several lasting relationships with men, quite apart from the "sex magick" rituals he performed with both sexes in later years. Indeed, he has said himself that relationships with prostitutes were easier and much more practical than lasting relationships with women, despite his having fathered several children by different women (two of whom he married) over the years.

We follow his initiation into the occult – which led him to meet the founders of the aforementioned "Hermetic Order of the Golden Dawn," an occult movement in London in the late 1890s. Several prominent figures of the day, including the poet William Butler Yeats and novelist Arthur Machen, were also members. This fascination with the occult continued throughout Crowley's life, leading him further and further up the hierarchy, until he finally crowned himself Ipsissimus of the Abbey of Thalema, the demon Baphomet.

There is no question at all that Crowley was a Satanist – widespread accounts (many firsthand) persist of his enactment of various rituals. However, there is also no doubt that he was a man of high intellect who refused to acknowledge limits in any area of his life – intellectual, social, or sexual. Unable to admit publicly to homosexuality (he was at university within a few years of Oscar Wilde's incarceration for the same), he was nevertheless known to be bisexual, something actively encouraged in rituals. During his lifetime he was accused of "immoral practices," including cannibalism, Satanism, and more; by his own admission, much of it was true. It is also true that he saw nothing wrong in his actions.

To those who think they know about Aleister Crowley – who think of him as "that Satanist," the man who called himself the Great Beast – there is so much more to learn. The film covers his life and his motivations in great detail, leaving the viewer with a much more rounded, "real" view of what the whole person must have been like. Certainly he was amoral, and certainly uninhibited – but he was also a man of great vision (whether or not that vision was misguided), many talents, and intellect. For anyone interested in truth, therefore, this film should be required viewing. Featuring narration by Joss Ackland, a score by Rick Wakeman, and able direction by Robert Garofalo, In Search of the Great Beast is available on DVD now.

The Eye

Starring: Jessica Alba, Alessandro Nivola, & Parker Posey
Review by Shawn Oetzel

Following in the footsteps of such films as The Ring and The Grudge, Lionsgate Film's newest vision of horror, The Eye, is based on a successful Hong Kong thriller. It is the story of a blind woman who, upon receiving a cornea transplant, finds her vision has not only been restored--but enhanced to the point where she has the ability to see into the supernatural world. As the tagline for the film suggests, "How can you believe your eyes when they're not yours?"

Jessica Alba stars as Sydney Wells, a concert violinist who has been blind since childhood due to a freak fireworks accident. With the aid of her sister Helen (Parker Posey), who, it is hinted, may have been the cause of the accident, Sydney opts to have a cornea transplant. What Sydney does not know is that the donor had the ability to see other peoples' deaths before they happened.

The operation goes off without a hitch, and according to all of the doctors is a rousing success. Sydney begins having side effects, however, which include images of a shadowy creature along with horrific visions of dying people. These are quickly dismissed by everyone including Dr. Paul Faulkner (Alessandro Nivola), the counselor whose job it is to help Sydney adjust to her newly restored sight.

Things quickly go from bad to worse as Sydney's visions intensify and her mental state begins to deteriorate. After imploring Dr. Faulkner to tell her who her donor was, Sydney and the doctor travel to the Mexico-based hometown of Sydney's donor. There Sydney learns of her donor's supernatural ability--and also discovers that her own visions are a warning from beyond the grave, of an impending disaster which Sydney must thwart.

The Eye is a decent film for anyone under the age of fourteen. Though I have never seen the film it was based on, I am fairly certain that this Hollywood version is extremely watered down. I believe the idea behind the story is good, but the execution left quite a bit to be desired.

Jessica Alba does a respectable job, but she just does not have the acting chops to pull off a lead role. In particular, she is not believable as a blind concert violinist. The scrip did not help her much either, as none of the characters were fully developed. This led to plot holes and confusion.

The movie does offer up several jump-out-of-your-seat scares which are fun, but as a whole left me disappointed. I would have liked to have seen less time spent on cheap scares and more time on character development. Being able to understand who these characters were would have helped this film immensely. If filmmakers are going to continue to adapt Asian horror films for American audiences, then they should use The Ring as the blueprint. If they do not, then unfortunately what we as the audience will be stuck with are unsatisfying movies such as The Eye.

Joshua

Starring: Jacob Kogan, Sam Rockwell, Vera Farmiga, Celia Weston & Dallas Roberts
Review by Shawn Oetzel

When I think of a family, it is usually a happy thought filled with children's laughter and the warmth of a home. However, what would happen if you removed the love or emotion --even from just one member? What would remain would be a cold and lifeless imitation of what a family should be. This is the essence of the film Joshua.

The Cairn family seems to have it all, especially after the birth of their daughter. Brad, the patriarch, is a well-to-do businessman with his beautiful wife Abby, gifted 10 year old son, and new baby girl. They all live in a large suite in an upper class New York neighborhood. Life seems to be absolutely perfect. That is, until things start to unravel.

Within days of bringing their new daughter home, the Cairns' son, Joshua, begins to distance himself. In the following days and weeks, the family falls completely apart as beloved pets start dying, baby Lily will not stop crying, and Abby slowly slips into madness. Brad works feveriously to keep his family from disintegrating, only to realize he himself has become a pawn in a 10-year-old boy's master plan to achieve the family he desires. In the end, Brad loses everything--including his freedom--as Joshua's plan comes to fruition.

Joshua is not your traditional horror movie. This is by no means a slasher flick or a movie that tries to scare you with cheap theatrics and overblown special effects. This is the creepiest kind of horror film, the dreaded psychological thriller. It plays on your mind by using a seemingly harmless young boy as an instrument of evil. It works against everything we hold dear, and that is why the movie will give you the chills.

The acting in Joshua is phenomenal, and its saving grace. Sam Rockwell is great as the father, and he does a magnificent job showing his character's descent into a world turned upside down. Vera Farmiga as Abby is fantastic as well. We learn early on that her character has a history of mental illness, and her descent into a complete breakdown--brought on by postpartum depression, as well as the devious scheme of her own son--is played to perfection by Ms. Farmiga. Then there is Jacob Kogan, who plays the title character. Not since The Omen has there been a creepier kid on film. His cold and calculating demeanor is the heart and soul of this film. Keep an eye out for this young man, because he has a bright future ahead of him.

This film is not for everyone. It is slow–paced, with very little action at times. The director, George Ratliff, takes a long time setting up the suspense, and these long interludes could turn some people off. The character development is superb, however, and the talent of each individual actor makes the film work. This is why I believe the film has picked up several awards at film festivals across the country, including a Best Feature award at the Gen Art Film Festival.

Joshua is billed as having a sort of "trick" ending. I believe this is somewhat misleading; to be honest, I found the ending to be fairly anticlimactic. This definitely takes away from the film, a time investment at 106 minutes. Do not get me wrong, it is not a bad ending, but with the build–up, you may feel let down by how everything plays out.

If you are a fan of horror films like Hostel, or any other of the blood and guts movies out there, then Joshua is not for you. People who like fast–paced, in-your-face horror will be deeply disappointed by this movie. However, if true psychological terror is your thing, then I suggest giving Joshua a try. The great performances from the entire cast help overcome a rather ordinary ending and make Joshua worth the investment.

◇◇◇◇◇◇◇◇◇◇◇◇◇◇◇◇◇◇◇◇◇

Gamers

Starring: Kevin Sherwood, Kevin Kirkpatrick, Scott Allen Rinker, Joe Nieves, Dave Hanson, and cameos by John Heard, Beverly D'Angelo, and William Katt
Review by Tim Deal

It was on some indie DVD a year or so ago that I saw the trailer for what seemed to be the ultimate in role-playing game (RPG) spoofs, *Gamers*. After failing to find the movie on Netflix or any of the brick and mortar movie rental chains I had assumed that the movie had failed to find distribution and thus fallen into obscurity. Then, this year in a period of serendipity, I began to reminisce about the joys of all-night *Dungeons and Dragons* (D&D) games with my friends and the adventure, fellowship, and Doritos that accompanied those nights. I was able to find the *Gamers*' web site (www.gamers-themovie.com) and I ordered a copy of the DVD.

I mention serendipity because not a month passed after I recalled my favorite D&D moments, when the esteemed founder of the game, E. Gary Gygax died, leaving many of his fans in sad bewilderment. Massive levels of geekiness clearly flows through our veins by the revelation that many of us saw Gygax as an icon of sorts—a grand master of our secret nerdy coven.

When the *Gamers*' DVD arrived, I watched it, perhaps unfortunately, with the lingering thoughts of Gygax on my mind. It was thanks to Gygax that a lonely awkward adolescent military brat was able to find an escape into mystic realms, and more importantly, find fellow travelers willing to accompany him there. So it was not without a candle burning for our beloved Gygax that I watched *Gamers* and hoped to find some nuggets of familiarity deep beneath the parody. Whether it was unrealistic expectations fueled by the loss of Gygax, or a monumental change in perspective spurred on by adulthood and early middle age, I am not sure. However what I am sure about is *Gamers*' inability to even remotely capture the very real and earnest humor brought about by the early days of the D&D phenomenon.

It seemed that the *Gamers*' crew gave up all hope of finding any humor in the subtleties of role-playing teenagers pretending to be elves and dwarves in the basement of their parents' home, and instead felt it necessary to assault the audience with a shotgun blast of over-the-top, outlandish and unrealistic, scene-chewing performances intended to elicit a laugh—all of this against the backdrop of a marathon Demon Nymphs and Dragons (DND—clever eh?) game.

The premise of Gamers is that five friends find themselves continuing a DND game that was launched 23 years earlier. Their ambition is to beat out a group of Iowa corn farmers (??) for the continuous DND-playing record. Here I was immediately mystified by the apparent ardent RPG-tendencies of the Iowa corner farmer. The friends consist of the Dungeon Lord (DL) Kevin (Kevin Sherwood) who reportedly penned 10 original songs for the film; Gordon (Kevin Kirkpatrick) whose parents are played by the talented John Heard and the anachronistically sexy Beverly D'Angelo; Paul (Scott Allen Rinker) who holds the group together and keeps their collective eyes on the prize, Fernando (Joe Nieves) and Argentinean who learns how to speak English by playing DND, and Reese (Dave Hanson) who is apparently the worst gamer in existence, insists on playing female elf cleric characters, and holds an almost psychotic grudge against the DL, Kevin, for killing his characters.

In addition to Heard and D'Angelo, there is a short cameo by William Katt (Greatest American Hero, House) who plays Reese's Madden Football-loving boss.

The set up is fine and the premise simple but effective. The film is shot in a documentary fashion (ala Christopher Guest's *Waiting for Guffman*, *Best in Show*, etc.) and the camera follows each of the characters on a few "day in the life" sequences that reveal their respective pasts, careers, and DND ambitions.

This is where the film deviates dramatically from its central theme. Writer/director Chris Folino (a former video game producer) felt the need to exaggerate his five principal characters to the point of disbelief in an attempt to out-funny the Farrellys, Apatow, and Herlihy combined. The result is a confusing ménage of horse husbandry, butchers clad only in athletic supporters, gay clown porn, and Dave Hanson's systematic devouring of the camera, crew, and craft services department as he vows vengeance on Kevin. Dave, please, relax!

As a fan of parody, I recognize the need for films of this nature to be rooted in believability. *Gamers* fails to do this on all levels, and as a result essentially gives the finger to an audience that wants nothing more than to find a reason to support the film.

Perhaps I am jaded by the loss of Gygax. Maybe the scores of positive blurbs that accompanied the DVD set my expectations too high. Or maybe I just don't need my laughs spoon-fed to me in a blatant attempt to win me over with its blatant silliness.

◇◇◇◇◇◇◇◇◇◇◇◇◇◇◇◇◇◇◇◇◇◇◇◇◇◇

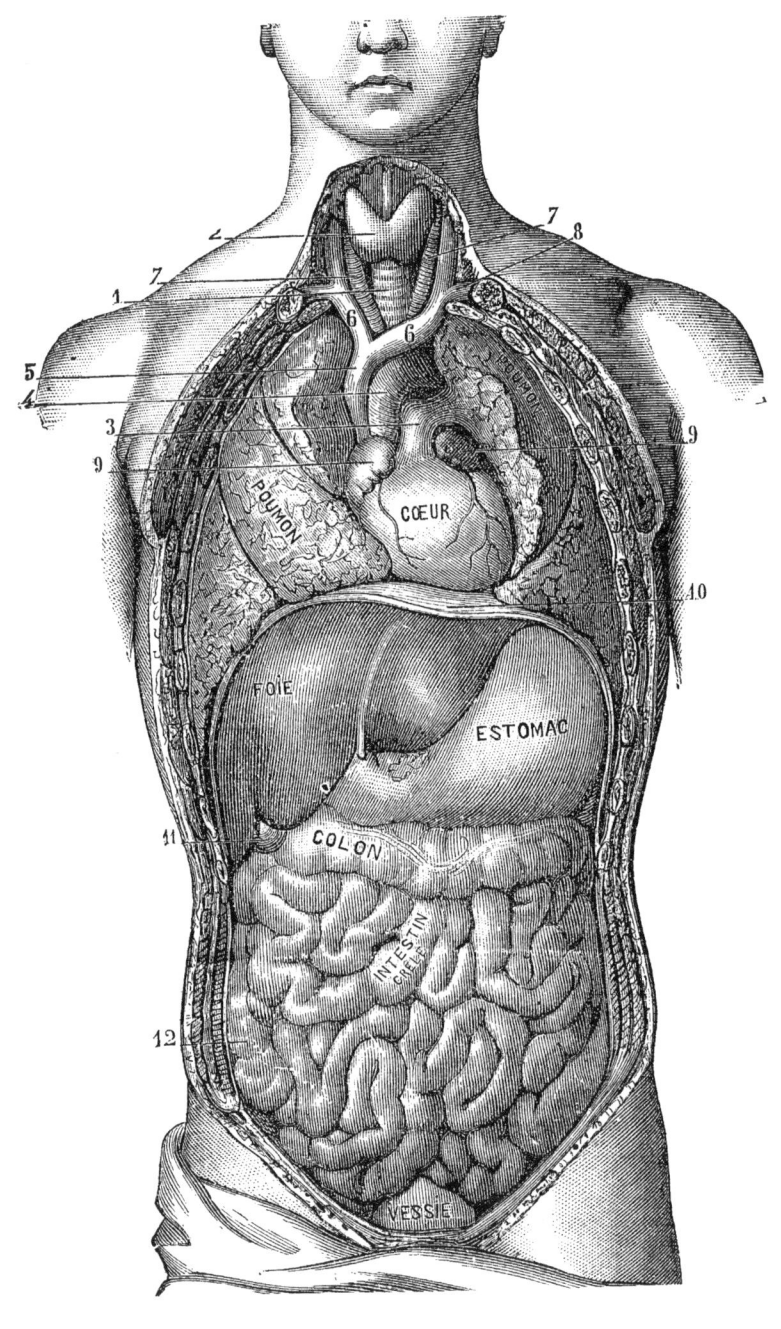

Dark Effigies
Artists Within the Genre

The Haunted Art of Thomas Straub
Tim Deal

Born as Norman Thomas Murphy, Dec 30th, 1963 in Vancouver, British Columbia. Given up for adoption, thus his name change as an infant.

He was adopted by an Air Force family, and grew up in a different city across Canada every few years, and Germany, near the Canadian base, CFB Baden.

London Ontario became Tom's home for many years staring in the early 80s, and after a couple of years living in Toronto, Los Angelas, and Calgary, London became his perminent residence.

He has always professed an interest in drawing, an attended the H.B. Beal Secondary art program known Nationally as Bealart, where he majored in films & animation. This, along with some adult classes years later at the same school, helped awaken the ability that Tom now uses in his imagery today.

Although a motivational dry spell killed his artistic desire earlier on, the computer and internet world opened up a new method and style.

Tom lives with his wife Tina, and three sons in London, travelling occasionally to conventions in Canada and the United States.

Tom is this issue's cover artist.

Q&A

Tim Deal: Who are some of your influences?
Tom Straub: Lewis Barrett Lehrman, artist of "The Haunted Studio". Tim Burtom, Walt Disney movies and the theme park Haunted Mansions, Illustrated ghost stories and comics from the 50s to present. Ghost towns and abandoned places, and old battlefields.
Tim Deal: What kind of art were you producing in your 7th grade art class?
Tom Straub: Lots of space ships, war-action, cartoon charactors, doodle galore. Nothing to right home about.
Tim Deal: What was/is your preferred media?
Tom Straub: Originally Was pencil crayon, oil pastel, acrylic. Photography and video can later, with photography and computers winning out in the end..
Tim Deal: Favorite 1980s teen comedy?
Tom Straub: No one favorite, but John Cusack 80s films ranked high with me.
Tim Deal: Favorite 1970s horror flick?
Tom Straub: Carrie !
Tim Deal: Name three things that absolutely terrify you.
Tom Straub: I refuse to answer, on the grounds that all three things might me used against me somewhere, someday... over and over...
Tim Deal: Can you give us the

evolution of your current technique?

Tom Straub: I started around 2003 or 2004, when collecting pictures for art reference files. There was a good photo of an old house, but with someone distracting in the photo. I tried erasing them in windows paint, but it didn't work. Then I tried copying and pasting bits around the person right onto them. It worked. The first couple of years everything was done with windows paint. Then I quite accidentally discovered that I had some software that came with our scanner, called Arcsoft PhotoStudio 5. It is a little program to edit pictures with. It took some of the pressure off using Windows Paint, and both programs work with each other to compensate for what the other doesn't have. I think I use about 10% or 15% of the functions from each program. The rest is not been figured out just yet. I have a Corel Draw 6 program gathering dust, and an Adobe Elements 6 I got last Christmas. Corel for me was too much to learn on my own, and the Adobe is going to need a bit of time I don't have right now to figure out also. I got it to help enlarge my images later to make the print stores lives a bit easier!

Tim Deal: Where do you find your subjects (people objects locations?)

Tom Straub: Early on when learning, a majority of images were a mix of Disney images off the internet, because I was

making fan art to add to bulletin boards like happy-haunts.com, and Doombuggies.com. When I figured out how to transfer my vhs camera videos to the computer, it made image selections a lot easier. Then as digital cameras got cheap, I got one, and have taken thousands upon thousands of photos over the years, averaging several hundred on my busiest days. My photos come from everything imagionable that I can get to. I'll take 13 hours to drive to an event six hours away, because I stop to take so many pictures along the way. People in my pictures are friends, family, neighbours, strangers, and Myspace volunteers. I once asked if some people wanted to be volunteer faces and bodyparts in my artwork, and the responce was so overwhelming, I had to stop the flood of images after a couple of days. Not only did I get people, but their houses, buildings, cars, trucks.... I still haven't sorted it all out, but the main folks are filed for when I need something or someone to work with. With some pictures, I've found them to not be usable, due to probable copyrights. I don't allow images to be sent to me anymore because I don't want to spent all my time hunting down unknown sources to verify usability. With the digital camera, I can come up with some nifty ways to create things.

Tim Deal: Tell us about your custom work. You can turn living people into ghosts?

Tom Straub: I prefer to work with real ghosts, but they take really crappy pictures ! Living people are much easier to work with. For those who want to be in a ghost work, I offer two ways. The $82 semi-commission, and the $300 regular commission. Those are the basic start prices. The Semi commission lets the person be added to an existing artwork, or added to just the background of an artwork I've made. I saved a lot of the backgrounds. That way, I just work the person only, and saves time. Full commissions get the works. People just wanting to buy prints can get them for $10-$20 each.

Tim Deal: Where can we expect to see your work in 2008?

Tom Straub: That's a hard question to answer. Events I'm looking into are:

A long term display is being made at the Haunted Mortuary in New Orleans.

ROLLING HILLS HAUNTED SANITORIUM East Bethany, NY. JUNE 12-15/08

HorrorHound Weekend Pittsburgh june20-22/08

Polaris 22, Toronto, July 11-13/08

Scarefest in Lexington KY, or UnivCon in Pennsylvania Sept 11-14/08

DragonCon Atlanta Georgia Aug.29-Sept 1/08

Context 21 Columbus Ohio sept 26-28/08

There are more I'm looking into. A couple may only have my art at the event, not myself. Considering The cost of attending events, and I have no money, it makes it a wee bit difficult. I'm looking into making a coffee table book of my work sometime. I have more than enough works for it. Getting traditional publishers to see it and consider it worthwhile is the biggest hurdle. I might try a small trial book thru a self publishing site, like Lulu's sometime, but that is a big IF! My plan is to also alter every picture for the book, so that they are not exactly the same as the prints people buy now, to keep them special. I already tend to change some artwork between printings, to try some improvement, different idea, and just because it's interesting to do. I make several or a dozen of each, and when sold, I might change them before printing off several more. Kind of my way to make the pictures special for the buyers at this early time in my "career".

You can learn more about Tom Straub and his haunted art by visiting him at: www.myspace.com/hauntedart.

***

Who is HIRAM GRANGE?

www.hiramgrange.com

Coming soon...

***

Puzzled
by I.E. Lester
Author Word Search

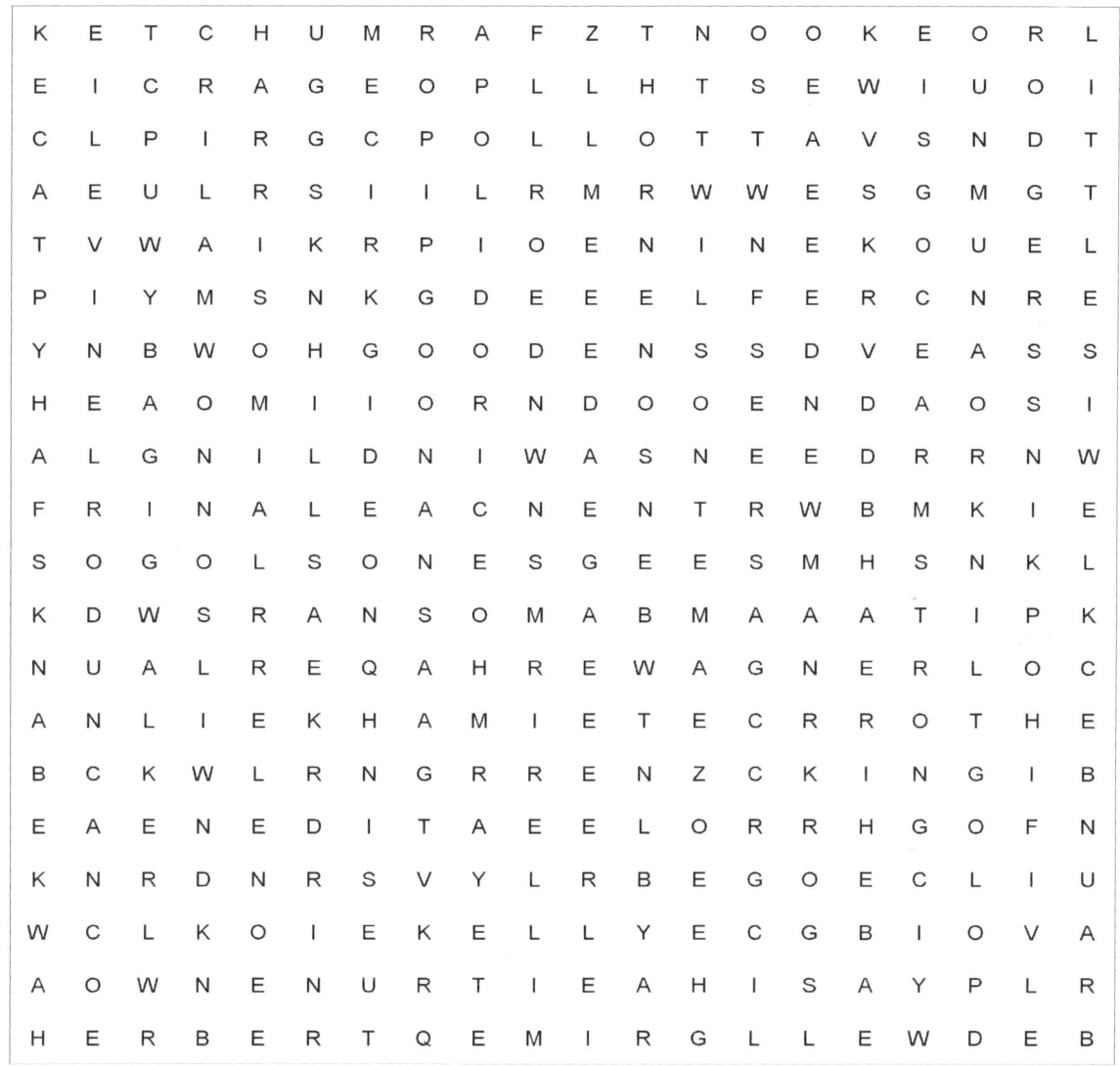

Last names only:
David Ambrose

Kelley Armstrong
L A Banks

Clive Barker
Stephanie Bedwell-Grime

E.F. Benson
Robert Bloch
Gary Braunbeck
Ron Dee
Tananarive Due
Lois Duncan
Cynthia Eden
pn Elrod
Thomas Fahy
Christopher Fowler
Stephen Gallagher
Nancy Gideon
Sephera Giron
Owl Goingback
Philip Gooden
Kathryn Ann Goonan
Muriel Gray
Stephen Hand
Thomas Harris
Simon Hawke
James Herbert
Joe Hill
Edward D Hoch
Nancy Holder
Brian A. Hopkins
Jack Ketchum
Stephen King
Tabitha King
Rudyard Kipling
Dean Koontz
Michael Laimo
Stephen Laws
Edward Lee
Tanith Lee
Ira Levin

Jeremy F Lewis
Herbert Lieberman
Kelly Link
Bentley Little
Marjorie M. Liu
Jeff Long
George R.R. Martin
Melinda Metz
Stephenie Meyer
Rex Miller
Christopher Moore
Simon Morden
Kim Newman
Mel Odom
Stewart O'Nan
Meredith Ann Pierce
John Polidori
Nick Pollotta
Kathryn Ptacek
Daniel Quinn
Hugh C Rae
Daniel Ransom
Simon Raven
Silver Ravenwolf
Kimberley Raye
James Reese
Anne Rice
Christopher Rice
Mary Linn Roby
Alan Rodgers
Savannah Russe
Jeffrey Sackett
John Saul
M.P. Shiel
John Skipp

Whitley Strieber
Melanie Tem
Tamara Thorne
Tim Waggoner
Karl Edward Wagner
Robert W. Walker
Mark West
f Paul Wilson
Robert Anton Wilson
Terri Windling
Douglas E. Winter

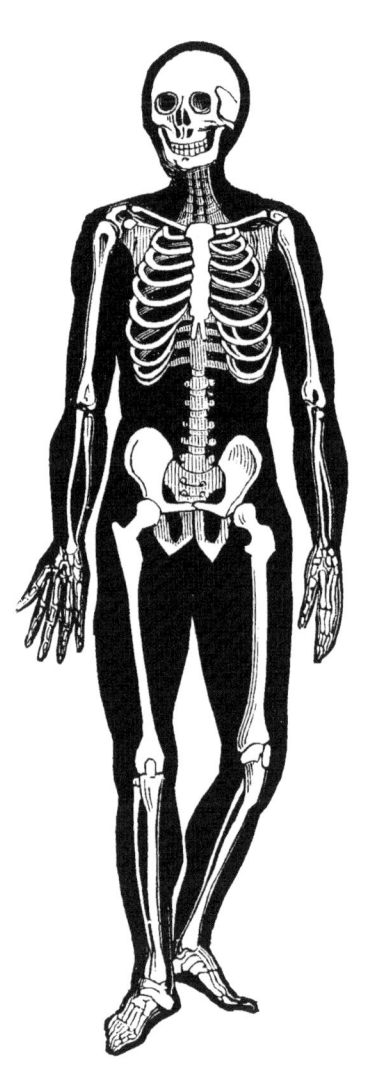

Shroud Submission Guidelines

Fiction: Shroud considers horror, dark mystery, dark fantasy and suspense short stories up to 5,000 words. In addition, we are interested in tightly woven flash fiction, and (in some cases) serialized novellas. Thriller and Suspense tales with a horror aspect are also welcome. We HIGHLY recommend that you buy a SAMPLE ISSUE in order to get a clear idea of our style and tone.

We are especially interested in:

Mythic horror in a real world setting; Classically-themed horror and suspense; Supernatural horror; Creature horror; Dark Fantasy in a contemporary/RW setting; Noir with a horror element.

We are LESS interested in:

Hard Science Fiction; Sword and Sorcery or anything set in a fantasy world; Stories about serial killers; Vampires ala Rice; First person accounts.

Submission Format: Send us electronic submissions in .DOC or .RTF format as a file attachment. Your subject line should clearly say "SUBMISSION". Simultaneous submissions are NOT okay. Please do not send us multiple submissions -- please only send us one story at a time and do not send your next submission until we give you a reply to the first. Reprints are fine provided they have not been published within three months and the author currently bears the copyright. A short bio would be nice, including any awards or published credits, however your story will stand on its own merit.

Response Time: Averages 2 to 4 months, but stories kept for further consideration by the editors may take additional time.

IMPORTANT: If you have NOT received an acknowledgment of receipt for your SHORT STORY within 1-5 Days of your submission then it is likely the submission was formatted incorrectly. We do appreciate your hard efforts and your creative vision, but with more than 350 submissions a month, if your submission is incorrectly formatted then it will be (unfortunately) deleted... sorry.

Artwork: Please query with samples. We are actively looking for talented artists for covers and B&W interior illustrations.

Nonfiction: Looking for well-researched stories on supernatural phenomenon, dark music, art, and interviews of key players within the genre, film reviews, game reviews. Query first. Payment .02-.03 cents a word.

Payment: Rates of .02 (most) to .05 (very few) cents per word, plus one contributor copy. Payable within 30 days of publication. Up to 5,000 words; maximum payment of $250. All rights revert to the author upon publication.

Anthologies: We automatically consider all fiction submissions for our active anthologies. If accepted, Shroud pays .01 cents a word plus two copies of the published collection.

Send To: editor@shroudmagazine.com

Novels and Novellas

Submission Guidelines (continued)

Shroud publishing is interested in building a catalog of intelligent dark fiction novels and novellas. If you have a COMPLETED manuscript or a series of short fiction, please query with a short synopsis and one sample chapter. Send to the editor.

A note on novel and novella submissions: we are a small press. We have a small press budget. If we are able to put your novel or novella into print we will do our best to market and distribute it, but the likelihood of you or us getting rich is very slim. Consider long and hard before you submit to us. We do not offer advances and our royalty rates will be modest. Having said that, if accepted, we will edit, design, layout your book, get it printed, sell it direct, and do our very best to get it distributed through a major distributor. WE will incur all of the aforementioned expenses, not you. We will never charge you for reading or publishing your book. Nor should you ever be.

So if this works for you, we'd love to see your novel/novella.

Response time for novels/novellas could be 3-6 months as our reading time permits.

***

For more information about Shroud please vist our Website at:

WWW.SHROUDMAGAZINE.COM

See our publications, join our forums, send suggestions, and more.

***

Made in the USA